THE SHADOW HUNT

THE SHADOW HUNT SERIES
BOOK 1

IAN FORTEY
AND
RON RIPLEY

EDITED BY ANNE LAO
AND DAWN KLEMISH

ISBN: 979-8-89476-281-4
Copyright © 2024 by ScareStreet.com

ENTER THE REALM OF TERROR...

We'd like to take a moment to thank you for your support and invite you to join our VIP newsletter.

Dive deeper into the darkness with exclusive offers, early access to new releases, and bone-chilling deals when you sign up at www.ScareStreet.com.

Let the nightmares begin…

See you in the shadows,
Scare Street

PROLOGUE

Droplets of blood splattered on the floor. Each one hit with a gentle thwap like a fat drop of rain. Solomon was trying to be quiet, but the flow of blood was not something he could control. The only way to silence it would be to slow down, and he could not slow down.

Sometimes, during a storm, the wind found its way through warped wood and moaned down the wide, empty hallways. It wound through cracks and crevices and groaned like a disembodied voice while the whole house creaked and shifted.

No storm raged outside that night. No wind snaked in through forgotten holes in walls to give voice to the empty passages and dusty rooms. It should have been quiet.

Solomon paused to listen, the flow of the blood from his wounds running down his body and saturating his clothes. Footsteps in the distance caused the distended floors to creak and squeal. The weight of a body sliding the wood up and down rusty nails was like an abrupt, inhuman shriek. Solomon waited as still as a statue, listening to where the sound came from and, more importantly, where it was going.

The noise of old hinges screaming as a door was opened in the opposite direction caused him to whip his head back. They were on both sides of him now. He was running out of places to go.

Solomon quietly made his way down an empty, unlit hallway to a set of stairs. He didn't want to risk leaving the house and exposing himself in the yard outside. He feared they would see him from the window, or that they had left someone outside to keep watch. The people pursuing him were thorough and relentless.

The basement of the house was pitch black. The power hadn't worked in years, and there were no windows. There was one way in and one way out. All he had to do was stay out of sight until they were gone. He could hide from them down there. There were a hundred shadows, a hundred more dark corners, and concealed places. He could hide from the devil himself down there.

He descended the steps without a sound. He was like a shadow, unseen and unheard. They would eventually come looking for him, but if he stayed hidden, they would give up. They had to.

Something thumped, and the sound was much closer than he expected. They would reach the stairs soon, and he needed to be elsewhere. He was good at hiding. They knew that, though.

The basement was partially finished. There were many rooms down there and a maze of hallways were littered with clutter. It had become something of a dump over the years, the forgotten corner of a forgotten spot, layered with memories of a dozen people's lives.

The basement dated from a time when nobody had basements. Before the invention of the steam shovel, it was almost unheard of for someone to dig out a foundation under their home. It must have taken many laborers weeks to clear the space under the house when it was built.

This was no mere root cellar. This was a fully functional floor with stone walls. It was made with a purpose. Later owners had no idea what that purpose was, but Solomon knew. Dark intent was worked into the building's structure from the ground up. He knew the basement was a good place to hide because it had been built as a place to hide things.

Boxes were stacked to the ceiling in some places, and there were shelves full of ancient lamps, dusty dinner sets, rusted tools, and crumbling books. Other corners were piled with decayed heaps of fabric, what had once been drapes and tablecloths and even tapestries. A fortune of ruin had been hidden away in the darkness, now home to dust and mildew and memories no one remembered.

Solomon weaved through the detritus looking for a spot where no one would think to look. A furnace was down there somewhere, and a well that was hundreds of years old. Hidden away behind a secret shelf, there was even a room where the stone walls had long ago been stained brown with the blood of too many people whose screams were never heard by those upstairs.

More hinges screamed, the door at the top of the basement stairs this time. Solomon moved faster, his eyes searching in the blackness of that horrible place until he settled on a passage that allowed for quick movement between rooms when someone didn't want to be seen. A secret passage once used to give a person the ability to spy unseen on the occupants down there.

Solomon crouched low and hid as best as he could. No one would know where to find him. No one alive knew of the passages, nor had anyone known about them for a century.

He heard the creak of footsteps coming down the stairs. Heavy feet, straining the wood as they descended. The stairs were weak and had not seen much use in decades.

Two people, Solomon thought. Maybe a third. He was unsure how many were in the house.

Once in the basement, they moved about quietly. The stone floor offered little opportunity for Solomon to hear his pursuers coming. He had to trust that they would have no luck in their hunt. He hadn't left a trail; he never did. He hadn't understood how they'd tracked him so far. How they'd tracked any of them.

Solomon strained to hear them. The hidden passage muffled sound, the thick stone providing insulation from the outer world in more ways than one. He had to trust that he would be fine.

He was alone now for the first time in a very long time. He couldn't remember the last time he had been by himself. The image refused to come to his mind. There was no time or place he could recall when he had been

3

alone. The others had always been with him.

There was a time when he wasn't in the house. He knew it in the way he knew the sun was on the other side of the world at night. Because he'd been told and because it made sense. But he had no proof. He had no firsthand experience. He couldn't remember ever being anywhere else. Not anymore.

Something metallic tapped on a wall. Solomon resisted the urge to move. Fear was there, buried in his gut like a living thing. He wanted to flee, to run from the house and across the yard to the distant trees. He wanted to run until he found that sun on the far side of the world, in some distant land he'd only read about long in the past. But that could never be. He was trapped.

The metallic thing tapped again. One, two, three times, like someone testing the stone. Solomon stayed where he was and waited. They weren't close yet. They were just looking. They were thorough; it was what they did.

When the strangers first arrived in the house, Solomon didn't know who they were or what they wanted. But he had always been cautious. He wasn't angry or confrontational. He held back and listened as they confronted Brewster.

Brewster owned the house. Or he had a long time ago. He still liked to think it was palatial, a mansion worthy of fine people with good social graces and solid upbringings. He never saw it as a rundown trash heap. And he hated trespassers.

Brewster approached them right away. threatened and howled like a wild animal. And they tore his head from his body.

Solomon had not seen anything like it in all his years. It was quick and so nonchalant, like no one even cared. Brewster's head came off like a cork in a wine bottle.

Chaos erupted then, and Solomon was not the sort to waste time. He had always been quick on his feet. So he fled. One didn't stop to ask for an explanation from people who removed heads, they just ran. So he ran.

He had heard them catch up with Lottie and how she begged for help for all of three seconds before her voice cut off with a sudden and final abruptness. He hadn't seen her, but there was no mistaking the sound. He knew he would never see her again.

These people, whoever they were, had come to destroy everyone in the house. They came to kill; it was as simple as that. They were hunters. And now he was the only one left.

More clicking. It was closer now—tap, tap, tapping its way. Was it some kind of tool? Did they have a way to see inside the walls? Surely not. It was impossible. But he would have thought pulling Brewster's head off was impossible, too.

He trusted his hiding place. He trusted his ability to be unseen and unheard. He was a shadow. He was a whisper. He was nothing. They would not find him.

Footsteps drew closer in the hallway beyond the passage. Only a wall of stone separated them.

"Reading a heat sink," someone beyond the wall said. Solomon made no sound. They would not find him.

"Bearing?" another voice asked.

Solomon was as still as the stone that surrounded him. He had no choice. He willed the strangers to move on, as though concentrating on the idea could force them away. They had to keep going.

"Here."

The voice was close, as close as it could get, right on the other side of the wall.

Something hit the stone hard, much harder than the tapping before. Mortar crumbled and stones fell inward. The end of a great, steel hammer burst through the wall above Solomon's head, and he cursed. How had they found him?

Solomon ran. His body passed through the stone of the wall, his eyes phasing briefly through gray nothingness and then coming out on the far side in a new passageway. It had been a long time since he had been afraid of anything. Since before he had died. But the things the strangers could do to the dead were unheard of.

He left behind the two men who had tracked him into the wall. Whatever modern technology they had or unique abilities, he didn't care. They could find him even when he was hidden, so he needed to get away. He needed to find a place where they couldn't go no matter what they had with them.

Solomon exited the next passage and appeared before the basement stairs once more. He would have to leave the house. It had been many years since he left the house, and he could only go so far. He was rooted to the house like all the others had been, even Brewster. But he still had options. There were still places he could go away from the house that might offer salvation.

One of the strangers had waited behind. She stood at the base of the steps, and when Solomon appeared in front of her, she smiled at him.

"Get out of my way," he ordered.

When Solomon had died, it had been the result of an attack by Brewster. The ghost had been in the house much longer than Solomon. He had tricked Solomon into thinking a window was a doorway. He had caused a pane of heavy glass to fall and nearly slice the top of Solomon's head clean off.

As a spirit, he was cursed with the brutal wounds he had received in life. The massive gash across his head bled eternally. He left a trail wherever he went. Thick, red blood followed him in a river, though it soon faded away in his absence.

Standing still, the gaping wound above his eyes exposed his skull and brain within. Blood flowed like a sheet down his face, and the image was terrifying. He could make it worse when he tried. He could make the blood of the living run cold as his gushed down his face in a torrent, the pools at

6

his feet moving as though they had a life of their own, seeking the warmth of living flesh.

"Or what?" the woman asked.

She carried no tools like the men, no technology or machines. There was a pistol in a holster at her side, but she did not draw it. Instead, she maintained her smile, waiting for Solomon to reply.

"I just want to leave," the ghost said, easing back on the intimidation. He did not have time to scare or harm the woman. He just wanted to go. "I don't want trouble with any of you."

"Hey," the woman said, her smile turning sympathetic. "I get it."

She reached out and rested a hand on Solomon's shoulder. He stared at it, unable to account for how he could feel her flesh touching his. It was neither warm nor cold, but there was a sense of pressure, something he had not felt in his entire existence as a ghost. She could touch him.

Her hand closed into a fist, bunching up Solomon's blood-stained shirt, and she yanked him off-balance toward her. She was swift as she turned aside, using the momentum of his sudden shift to throw him to the ground at her feet.

"I don't want to hurt anyone," Solomon called out as he hit the ground at the base of the stairs.

"I do," she replied.

The amusement in her voice was striking, cold, and terrifying. Solomon was face-down at the base of the steps, and the woman was quick to jump on him. He could feel her weight pinning him down. He felt a knee in his back and then hands on his head. He struggled to move, to right himself, but he was unable to. She was too strong, and he didn't understand how.

Solomon felt her hands on his head. She forced it to turn, jerking it quickly. There was a crunching sound and something broke. The woman twisted his head all the way around and he tried to scream, not in pain but in shock and terror, only nothing came out.

Her hands pushed down harder on either side of his skull. He heard it beginning to break, a single crack, and then he heard nothing else.

✻ ✻ ✻

Tully and Kraft were loading the back of their truck with gear while Beatrix smoked a cigarette outside of the house. She was trying to get the smell of the basement out of her nose, a mix of rotten fabric and mold that clung like a mask on her flesh.

Lanthimos came out of the house carrying his case and paused next to her. He balanced the aluminum on the rickety banister and popped it open, reaching inside to pull something out.

"Yours," he said, holding out a smashed pocket watch. She held the cigarette between her lips and plucked it from the thin man's hand. The inner workings were mangled and fused in some places. Springs and gears and tiny rods were bent and warped, and the glass from the face was all but gone.

She guessed the watch was at least a hundred and fifty years old, maybe older. Beatrix was hardly an expert in antiques. Most of what she knew was from what she did, stuff that had rubbed off over the years.

"Nice. Last one?" she asked.

"Solomon Zaslav," Lanthimos said, reading from a notebook. "Owner from eighteen sixty-two until eighteen seventy-seven."

"Murdered?"

"Accident," he said. "Window fell on his head."

She laughed and tossed the watch back at him. He caught it awkwardly but managed to not drop it.

"Put it with the other crap. We've got to get going. Next stop is Manchester."

Lanthimos did as instructed, dropping the watch back in the case with other destroyed items before closing the case.

Beatrix quickly finished her cigarette and then flicked the butt at the house's broken front door. She was ready to find a bar and have a drink.

CHAPTER 1
A STRANGER

The bell above the door jingled as someone entered the shop. James Moran intended to lift his head and see who it was, but he was caught up reading a document about a ghost that had haunted a Shinto shrine in Japan. It was said to have decapitated more than one hundred people at the turn of the previous century. It was a firsthand account from a Shinto kannushi, and the entire account was written in remarkable detail while being simultaneously even-handed and neutral of language in a way he'd never encountered. It was spellbinding.

"Welcome to Moran and Moran," he said without looking up.

"Hard at work, Mr. Moran?" a familiar voice said playfully.

James looked up in time to see Brent, the neighborhood postman, put a stack of letters and several small parcels on the counter. Brent had come into the shop almost daily for about five years. They never had long conversations, and James didn't even know the man's last name. But they were always cordial in the way people are when they see each other regularly and had developed a casual familiarity in their interactions.

"Always, Brent. You?"

"The mail never stops," the man said. "Got two you need to sign for today."

James frowned as Brent handed him an electronic pad and a stylus pen so he could sign his name on a touch screen. He didn't like signing his name using such gadgets as it never looked like his real signature, and he felt like it cheapened the process. But it was a small thing to worry about, nothing more than a pet peeve that he never voiced to anyone else, but he still thought of it every time he had to sign for a new package.

"See you around," Brent said, taking the electronic pad away.

"Yes, have a good day," James said, absently looking over the new mail.

He was eager to get back to the tale of the Shinto spirit, but he felt like it was probably a better idea to at least look over the mail he'd received in case there was anything pressing he needed to take care of.

The stack of envelopes included several bills, notices, and solicitations for services he had no interest in. Instead, he focused his attention on the two packages, neither of which were expected.

The first was an overstuffed manila envelope, and the interior was full of images of various antiques. The letter that accompanied it was from Mrs. Aubrey Kazmarek, a client of the antique side of the business who had a bad habit of sending clippings of all the antiques she came across that she wanted. Many of the items were of historical significance and impossible for anyone to own, but she still sent them no matter how many times James assured her she could not buy pieces from palaces or museums.

The second package came from someone James did not recognize. E. Pearl in Manchester was the return address. James might have known them, but it didn't ring a bell.

The phone drew his attention from the package, and he set it aside. After his call, James found his way back to the story of the Shinto ghost and forgot about the parcel until it was time to close shop at around five in the afternoon.

He took the package and the rest of his mail into his office at the back of the store and set it on his desk. He filed away the important mail in the appropriate places and shredded the rest for recycling. He included Mrs. Kazmarek's photos of well-known antiquities in his recycling pile.

The Manchester package did not weigh much, and it was compact. He opened it and pulled out a small box, the sort someone might use to house a locket as a gift. There was no note attached and nothing to indicate who E. Pearl was or what they wanted.

Suspicious, James placed the sealed box on his desk. It was not unheard of for people to send him haunted items. In fact, it happened often. But when it happened, it was nearly always prefaced by a call, or some arrangement that required prior notice.

James crossed the room and took a heavy, flat box off a shelf near his filing cabinet. There was nothing outwardly remarkable about the box. It was plain, made from pine, and had a very basic latch on it. But the box was heavy because of the lead plates that lined the inside. From time to time, he used it to store small, haunted items when they needed to be transported without the ghost attached to them causing a fuss.

With the lead-lined box open on his desk, James carefully loosened the top of the small box he'd received and dumped the contents into the lead receptacle. His hand rested on the lid, ready to drop it at the slightest provocation. The weight of the lead plate on top would make it slam shut in the blink of an eye if anything threatened him.

A single silver dollar dropped from the box with a clink onto the lead plate. The coin was old, dented, and tarnished, and it was stamped with the year 1902. It was probably worth thirty dollars. He could see nothing special about it, and as an antique, it was not worth his time. But he already knew that was not why it had been sent to him.

The room was still. He waited a beat to see if anything would materialize, but nothing happened. He tentatively reached out his hand and let the tips of his fingers hover above the coin. The temperature change was subtle but noticeable. The coin was unnaturally cold. The hallmark of a haunted item.

"You have a choice, friend," James said, pulling his hand away. "I can seal you in this lead box and maybe unearth you in a year or two if I remember you're in there, or you can come out now and let me know why you were sent here."

He waited for a reply, and for a tense moment, he thought the ghost might choose imprisonment. But it only lasted a moment.

"Please, Mr. Moran. I'm just looking for help."

The ghost stood in the doorway to the office, a respectful distance from James. He manifested as a young man, probably in his early twenties. His hair was chestnut brown and hung in loose curls, and James imagined there was a time when girls would have found him attractive. That time was probably before whatever had smashed in the left side of his face.

The injury was substantial and hideous to look at. Something of either great mass or great speed had collided with the side of his head and crushed his skull. James saw fragments of skull and brain mixed with the blood and ruined flesh. It was one of the more graphically unpleasant injuries he'd seen in a spirit, and he'd seen many.

"Okay. And you are?" James asked.

"My name is August," the ghost replied. His voice was gentle and reminded James of one of those boy-band singers kids seemed to be into. Or they had at one time; he wasn't sure if that was still a cultural phenomenon. The ghost's accent was from New England, but not very pronounced. "I used to be part of a collection that belonged to Benedict Winston."

James didn't react except to nod slightly. Benedict Winston was a name he recognized. The old man lived in Manchester and had been an occasional client of James'.

Winston was not as wealthy as other collectors of haunted items, and he didn't obsess over it as much as some did. Years ago, he had purchased a couple of items from James but nothing significant. He was not one of those men who wanted to have the ghost of Lincoln or an ancient king. He was more interested in what a ghost did, or was good at, in life.

James had provided him with one spirit that was passingly good at playing chess, and another that had once been a Broadway actor. Winston wanted someone who could perform Shakespeare for him. But James was not familiar with the ghost speaking to him.

"I haven't heard from Mr. Winston in about ten years," James said.

August nodded.

"No, sir. He had stopped collecting some time back. I think he had as many friends as he felt he needed."

"Friends?" James asked.

August smiled almost sheepishly.

"Well, sure. We were his companions. He was a lonely man. He liked to play chess and watch movies. I taught him how to cook."

"You cook?"

"I was a chef. I trained in France for two years. Never won a James Beard Award or anything, but I could make a good ceviche, and Mr. Winston enjoyed my recipe for Beef Wellington."

"Interesting," James said. "But I noticed you refer to him in the past tense."

August nodded, the gesture causing blood to flow more freely from the wound on his left side. While James watched, the drops ran down the ghost's face and then faded away before they dripped from his jaw to his shoulder.

"Mr. Winston is dead. That's why I came to you for help. The people who killed him are looking for me."

James had never been close with Winston, but he seemed a nice enough man. He was in his seventies when James knew him and had a strange, almost childlike curiosity about the world of the dead. It made some sense that he had collected spirits to be his friends. He was socially awkward and probably didn't relate well with living people.

As far as James knew, Winston didn't have any family. He'd never married, had no children, and seemed to live exclusively off money that he'd made from investments many years earlier. His life was devoted to his hobbies, and he seemed very fulfilled by that.

"Who killed him?" James asked.

"He called them... Harvesters? *The* Harvesters? He knew them somehow. I heard them talking before it happened," August explained.

"It wasn't just one person that killed him?"

The ghost shook his head.

"Five that I saw. I ran when I saw what was happening. They didn't just kill Mr. Winston, they killed almost everyone. They were after all of us," he said, his voice low as though he feared someone might overhear.

"What does that mean? Who else was killed?"

"The other ghosts. Mitchell and Otani and Silva. They killed them all."

August had grown very quiet. He had yet to move from the doorway to the office, and more than his words, his body language showed the fear he felt. Though James was not sure what August had witnessed, it had shaken him.

"I'm afraid I'll need you to explain that to me. These... Harvesters, they killed ghosts?" James said.

August nodded, staring at the coin in the lead box.

"They had tools. Machines of some kind. They were tracking us. Hunting us. And there was a woman. She was the only one I saw do it. She caught up with Otani. That was the chess player; do you remember her?"

"I do," James said. He vaguely recalled the name, but the ghost was one James had found for Winston. She was exceptionally good at chess and seemed to have little interest in much else. Winston was thrilled with her.

"Otani saw Winston dead, and she was so angry. She was cursing them out, and I'd never seen her angry. But this woman approached her, and she touched her. She laid hands on her. I'd never seen anything like it. She took Otani's face in her hands. It almost looked tender for a moment, like she was going to kiss her. But then her arms tensed and flexed."

"You're sure this woman could physically touch the spirit?" James asked.

August met James' gaze.

"Oh yes. She tensed, and Otani screamed but only for a second. And then, her head crumbled. Her body just burst, you know? Came apart. And then she was gone. The living woman killed her. Have you ever seen anything like that?"

James did not answer. He needed to learn more from August.

But of course he had seen something like that before.

CHAPTER 2

ESCAPE

"How did you get away?" James asked.

August shook his head and looked at the coin.

"Winston didn't keep that with the rest of them. Everything was in a safe in his office, but the coin was in his car. He used to take me shopping so I could help him pick ingredients. I ran when they were killing everyone. I ran as far as I could go, and I hid for a day. The safe was cleared out when I got back. They'd taken everything. But I knew they'd be back, so I had to leave."

"How did you accomplish that? I've never seen a ghost mail itself," James said.

"Mrs. Pearl. She's our neighbor. She could see us. We found out by accident many years ago. Mr. Winston talked to her and introduced us, and eventually, she came to understand I'm not as awful as I look. I helped her cook sometimes."

"I see," James said. "You directed her to the coin."

"I told her to find your address. I'd heard Mr. Winston talking to you in the past. When he got Otani and Silva. I knew you knew about us, and you could help ghosts get from one place to another. You're the only person I could think of to help me. They're still looking for me. They might have killed Mrs. Pearl too if I stayed with her. I need you to hide me."

James nodded, considering the ghost's words. He was confident enough now that the ghost was not going to be dangerous. He pulled his chair and sat down, contemplating what to do next. He didn't think he would need to trap August in the lead box, but he still needed more information before he could decide what to do.

"How do you know these Harvesters are still after you? Why would they be?"

"They came for us. I heard them arguing with Mr. Winston before he was killed. They wanted all of us."

"They said that? Precisely?"

"They were there to hunt us, the ghosts. They didn't even know Mr. Winston. I think one of them did, but the woman and the others didn't even care that he was there. Then they just shot Mr. Winston. It was us they wanted."

James had heard of people seeking out ghosts; that was not unusual. There were many dangerous collectors in the world, people who engaged in shady and underhanded practices to get what they wanted. Some, like the Cult of the Endless Night, seemed to have no qualms about committing theft or murder to achieve their goals. But the Harvesters were something new. He had not even heard chatter of such a group through his usual contacts.

"You said these Harvesters destroyed the spirit Otani. Did they capture some of the others?"

"They were hunting us, Mr. Moran. It wasn't about catching; it was what you said—destroying. They wanted to destroy us. I don't think they cared about me and Otani that much. They wanted the thing in the box."

The words hung in the air for a moment before James said anything. August had said it casually like it made all the sense in the world, but James needed to know more.

"What's the thing in the box?" he asked.

"I don't know," the ghost replied.

James sighed and leaned back in his chair.

"I need you to help me with this, August. Your story isn't making a lot of sense to me. It will be hard to help you if I don't understand what happened and who these people are. So what do you mean by 'the thing in the box'?"

"Mr. Winston collected things. I don't know what it was, I swear. He never opened it. But these Harvesters… they wanted it. A lot."

"But how do you know these things? What did they say to you?"

"To Mr. Winston," August corrected. "I was already hiding. And it was the woman with them, the one who could harm us. She said they just wanted to hunt it down. That one of the men paid to hunt it down."

"It?"

August huffed and shook his head, growing frustrated.

"I wasn't there at first, okay? I didn't hear it all. I didn't see them show up. I didn't hear how it started or how things got so bad. I just know they wanted something, and a man paid to hunt it. She said that specifically. She used the word 'hunt'."

"So, these Harvesters are hunting outfitters? They provide the gear and expertise for a person to hunt spirits?" James asked.

"That's what it seemed like," August agreed.

"How did they know about Winston's collection?"

"I don't know," August said, sounding tired and exasperated. "He knew some people. Others who had ghosts. He didn't tell me everything. We spent time together when he wanted to cook; that was all. I was just there to help him cook."

"It's fine, I understand," James said to calm the spirit. "You got away already though, you understand that, right? I can't imagine they'll be after you."

"You don't know that," August said, shaking his head. "I went back the next day because I thought they had to be gone, but they weren't. The safe was emptied and they took everything, but they came back when I was there. They knew I had returned, and they came back for me."

"What else was in the safe?"

"Just Otani and Silva and Mitchell's items. And the box that held what they wanted."

James considered his words carefully. There were questions about the Harvesters and no easy answers. If they were hunters, why would they have emptied Winston's safe? James knew that when a ghost was destroyed in that fashion, it ruined the haunted item that the ghost had been linked to.

"They took the items that belonged to Otani and the other spirits? Are you sure they were all destroyed?"

"I saw it happen," August insisted.

It did not make sense. The items would have been ruined; why take them? What good was a destroyed pocket watch or pendant, or bag of bones that had been reduced to rubble? And why would they come back for a ghost like August? Even if they were hunting for sport, what sport would come from destroying a timid former chef?

"I have to be honest with you, August, none of this makes sense to me."

"You think it made sense to me?" the ghost replied. "Mr. Winston was eighty-three years old. He could barely walk. He never hurt anyone, never did anything. They murdered him and then they murdered our friends. It doesn't make any sense."

James said nothing. The ghost was angry, and rightfully so. Sometimes, madness was its own explanation. Not that he thought these Harvesters, as organized as they sounded like, were mad. But their motives were obviously not meant to be understood by others. Some people thrived on chaos and destruction, and that was justification enough for any actions.

James Moran had only ever heard of one person in the world who could do what August said these Harvesters could. James had to call Shane Ryan and let him know what had happened. Someone out there doing what he could do, hunting ghosts and murdering people who got in their way, was something he suspected Shane would not stand for.

"If these people are still after you, August, I don't know that there's much I can do to help you myself," James said.

The ghost's expression darkened, and he finally took a step into the room.

"Please, there's no one else. They hunt ghosts; it's what they do. Just send me to someone. Send me to another country. I don't care where. There must be a place I can go," he said desperately.

James raised his hands to calm the ghost.

"Don't despair just yet. I don't know if I can help you personally, but I might know someone who can. I have a friend whose skills will be more beneficial in a case like this."

"What skills?" August asked.

"Skills in dealing with people like this. Even if I found a place to send you, it might not dissuade these Harvesters from coming after you or others like you. That's the problem my friend can help you with, but he's going to need information from you. He might even need you to show him some things. Are you willing to take on a risk like that?"

"These people are dangerous, Mr. Moran," August whispered.

"As is my friend," James countered.

August seemed reluctant, but after a moment of thought, he nodded.

"I'll help if I can," he said.

It was still early in the evening, and James didn't think he would be disturbing Shane to give him a call at that hour. He didn't like to call anyone outside of business hours as it was generally impolite to do so, but he thought this was something Shane would want to know about.

James also wanted to see if he could find out who else Benedict Winston did business with. August had not come through the shop, so Winston had at least one other supplier of spirits.

The ghost made it clear that at least one person with these Harvesters knew who Winston was. Someone knew that he collected ghosts and was bold enough to come to his house to hunt them down. Whatever perverse pleasure they got from destroying spirits, or watching someone else destroy them, it was not something that others in the community would support.

Most of the clients he dealt with spent a lot of money to curate their collections. Those people would not have taken kindly to learning that they were now at risk of phantom trophy hunters who were willing to kill the living to have a chance at the dead.

If someone was out there hunting ghosts, word had to be traveling, even if it was still deep underground. The way August described it didn't make it seem like this was the Harvesters' first job. No one came up with a name like the Harvesters on a whim, either. These people were organized and had done this before. Someone had to know about them.

"Would you mind terribly if I closed you up for some privacy while I make a call?" James asked. "This is a sensitive subject, after all."

"In there?" August asked, pointing at the lead-lined box.

"Just for a few moments," James said.

August stared at the box. The blood from his wound oozed slowly, a perpetual cycle of it flowing, dripping, vanishing then oozing again.

"Just don't leave me there for long."

"No, of course not," James said. He paused, his hand on the box lid, and then pulled away.

"Why don't you go out into the shop for a minute instead? Look around if you like. I'll let you know when I'm done."

"Sure, okay," the ghost agreed. He left without any further prompting and James got his phone out.

He speed dialed Shane Ryan's number.

CHAPTER 3

GROUNDWORK

Shane Ryan lit a cigarette and stared at August over a cup of steaming, black coffee. James Moran sat to his left. None of the house ghosts were in the room, but he knew they were nearby, listening in.

Eloise had expressed some excitement when James had shown up at the door. It had been some time since any visitors had come to Shane's house, especially any who had stayed long enough for a cup of coffee. Eloise never liked to show that she was pleased when someone came over, and she could easily shift her moods into anger that someone was invading her space, but it was clear how she felt when she saw James.

On the other hand, once she realized that James had brought a ghost with him, she made herself scarce. Shane suspected she was in the walls, maybe in a passageway or even in a vent somewhere, observing everything.

Carl had been more polite. He had said hello to James and offered a curt nod to the spirit he brought with him before excusing himself and taking the Davis sisters and Thaddeus with him.

Only Herbert remained visibly in the area, waiting patiently in the next room as though it were a doctor's office, and he was hoping for his turn to speak to Shane. He had not been in the house long enough to develop the strange quirks the others had when people showed up. Having more worldly experience than the other ghosts, Herbert was very open to new people and new things.

"Tell me they didn't seriously call themselves the Harvesters," Shane said.

"The woman with them called them that," August replied. "The one talking to Mr. Winston. She said one of the men with her paid the Harvesters a lot of money, and he expected a real hunt. She sounded amused, but I don't know why."

"You saw her, or you heard her?" Shane asked.

"Heard. I wasn't in the room. Mr. Winston didn't like any of us to be in a room with company unless we were invited. He feared someone seeing one of us by mistake."

"Reasonable," Shane said. He took another drag from the cigarette and nodded to James.

"You told him you saw the woman destroy a ghost. Describe it."

"I saw her kill Otani, yes. She just gripped her head. Squeezed it until it burst. And I heard Mitchell and Silva go. It sounded like an explosion."

Shane glanced at James but said nothing.

"Did any of you fight back?"

August scoffed.

"I know what I look like, Mr. Ryan, sir. It's not pleasant. But I'm not a monster. I've never hurt anyone. I was never even in a fistfight when I was alive. And like this… what do ghosts even do to people? Rattle chains and show them Christmas past?"

Shane frowned.

"You don't get out much, huh."

"I do. We went grocery shopping every week at Whole Foods."

Shane sighed and took a sip of coffee.

"Never mind. So none of you were fighters, and these people destroyed three spirits and stole a box?"

"It wasn't just a box," August explained. "It was a ghost."

"You told me you didn't know what was in the box," James interjected. August looked vaguely sheepish.

"I don't know who it was, but I know it was a ghost. Mr. Winston never opened it while I was there. I don't think he even touched the box in all the years I was with him."

"Then how do you know what was in it?" Shane asked.

"Mr. Winston talked about it once on the phone. The box was made of lead like the one Mr. Moran has, but nicer. It was decorative. He kept a ghost inside that was too dangerous to be let out and too dangerous to entrust to anyone else."

"Winston said this?" Shane asked.

"On the phone," August confirmed. "It was a long time ago. But he was afraid of what was in the box and never wanted to have it opened again. Not by him or anyone."

"And the Harvesters stole it," Shane said, taking another puff of his cigarette.

August shook his head.

"No, sir," he said.

Shane sighed and raised an eyebrow, glancing at James again.

"You're starting to talk in circles here, bud. They took it or they didn't, it can't be both."

"They didn't steal it," August explained. "They let it go."

The admission was unexpected. Shane took another drink of coffee and then gestured to the ghost to keep going.

"It was the one they wanted most, from what I heard. The others and I weren't a big deal. I think we were in the way more than anything. You could tell the woman was disappointed when she killed Otani. She made some crack about there being no fight."

"No fight?" Shane repeated.

"Yes, sir. She wanted Otani to try harder. To fight back or something."

"She wanted it to be sporting."

"Maybe," August said. "But the thing in the box was what they wanted. I heard one of them question the others. He asked what the point was if they couldn't get 'him'. He seemed upset. Then the woman told him to calm down, and that they'd set him loose soon enough."

"Set him loose," James said. "They wanted to hunt this dangerous ghost even though they had access to its haunted item? They didn't need to hunt it if they had it captured."

"They don't want to capture it," Shane said. "They want to fight it. They want to see if they can outsmart it and overpower it. This woman wants to see it with her eyes. She wants to watch it crumble in her hands."

In a way, Shane understood what the Harvesters were doing. He had destroyed enough ghosts in his time, endured fights that took him within an inch of his life. There was a feeling that he didn't suspect many people in the world would understand. That feeling when he triumphed over a spirit, when he crushed that ghostly flesh in his hands and felt the energy surge outward and wash over his body as it was destroyed. He could see someone chasing that feeling, seeking it out on purpose.

If this woman was a true trophy hunter the way someone who went on a safari in Africa in search of a lion was, she wanted the danger. She wanted to feel the risk and know there was a chance she would be the one who died at the end of the hunt. Maybe she found a way to make money off it by bringing along tourists. But she was the center of this. She was the engine that made the machine work.

"So they've released a killer somewhere and seek to hunt it and destroy it just for fun," James said. "That's novel."

"It's something," Shane agreed.

Shane's first instinct was to question what kind of person would fund an operation like that, but he quickly pushed that out of his mind. He had run afoul of too many groups with too many wealthy people interested in burning that wealth in the pursuit of the most dangerous or unusual ghost. This was just a repackaged version.

The Iron Tournament wanted the living and dead to fight each other. The Reapers wanted to be paid to do mercenary work. The Cult of the Endless Night wanted to gather the rarest spirits in the world. The Harvesters just wanted to hunt them down and destroy them for fun. Why not? The living were just as macabre as the dead, the only difference was they tended to do it for money.

"When I came back the next day, and I thought the Harvesters were gone, I saw that they had taken the box from the safe. When they came back looking for me, I heard them talking. Whatever was in the box got away from them, too. They let it loose somewhere, and they hadn't found it."

Shane lowered his cigarette and gave the ghost a considering look.

"When did you mail yourself to James?"

"Three days ago," he answered. "I had Mrs. Pearl send it priority."

"Three days," Shane said. He looked at James. "Have you heard anything about Winston's death?"

"I have not," the older man answered. "There was nothing in the local media, but he had no family that I know of to contact."

"There was no one," August confirmed. "I told Mrs. Pearl, when I asked to be mailed to you, Mr. Moran, but also warned her not to tell anyone. For her safety."

"So he could still be there," Shane said. "It's possible no one even knows he's dead."

"The Harvesters could be using the house as a base. Hunting this dangerous spirit if they haven't captured it yet," James agreed. "But why not take it elsewhere? Why risk getting caught?"

"You don't import a lion to hunt it in New Hampshire," Shane said. "Keep the beast where it is. Hunt it where it fits in, give it every advantage. Then, when you bag it, you prove your superiority."

"But this is not a wild animal," James said. "If what August says is true, this is a dangerous and calculating killer loose in a residential area with people who have no way to defend themselves."

"Exactly," Shane said.

He knew on some level that James understood, but James was often focused on what seemed practical or even sensible over some of the crazier things people in the world did. Shane understood the bloodlust and recklessness. The thrill of it all. The Harvesters didn't care about anyone. They wouldn't care if people died. If anything, that would add to the thrill of the hunt.

"We should call the police, don't you think?" August said. "For Mr. Winston's body. And for Mrs. Pearl and others in danger."

Shane stared at the ghost and frowned. He was definitely a chef and not someone who spent a lot of time dealing with dangerous people.

"These people strike you as the type to listen to the police?" Shane asked.

"It doesn't matter if they listen," August countered. "The police will arrest them, and then you and Mr. Moran can find the thing in the box and store it safely."

Shane finished his coffee and set the cup on the table. He ran a hand across the top of his head and found himself wishing it had just been another quiet day at home.

"These people came in and shot your friend. They can destroy the dead. They have gear and intel and at least some kind of strategy. If the cops show up, they're either going to find an empty house with no sign of these people, or they're going to join your pal Winston in the dirt. Either way, bad way to solve a problem."

"And the police are also at risk of getting hurt by this ghost," James added.

August looked nervously from Shane to James.

"Then what are we going to do? No offense to you or Mr. Ryan, but when you said you had a friend who could help, I thought you meant the police, or a federal agent, or someone with power."

Shane chuckled and got up from the table, taking his cup to the sink to wash it.

"Yeah, James, why didn't you take him to someone useful?"

"Trust me, August, Shane is the man for the job. If anyone can find the ghost they released and stop them from doing it again, it's him," James said.

"Don't gas me up too much. Makes me look bad if I screw up." Shane chuckled again.

He rinsed off the cup and then dried it and put it back in the cupboard before turning back to face the ghost.

"We should get going," he said. "Before anyone else dies."

CHAPTER 4

THE BOX

Shane and James stood outside of Shane's house under the bright morning sun. August was between them, pacing and looking anxious, but both living men ignored him.

"I can dig up some information on these Harvesters," James said, unlocking the door to his car. "If they are taking people on hunts for money, someone must have heard of them by now."

"Let me know what you find. In the meantime, we'll go check in on Winston's house, see how things look," Shane said.

August stopped pacing and looked from James to Shane.

"*We'll* go? You mean you and me?" he asked.

"You know the place," Shane said as though it were obvious.

August turned to James, looking desperate.

"I went to you to get away. Away from there! You're going to send me right back?"

"Shane will help you, August, but he has to look into this. He can't just make these people disappear."

"But they're after me. They're going to kill me if I go back!"

"Try to be optimistic. Maybe we'll kill them first," Shane said.

August looked horrified.

"Trust him, August. Or trust me, at least. You came to me for help, and this is the best help I can think of," James said reassuringly.

August's hands were balled into fists, and he looked like he might scream as he took to pacing again.

"I thought you'd be able to do something. It's like you haven't heard a word I said. There's a woman who can kill ghosts! Don't you understand what that means? She can kill them with her bare hands. People aren't even supposed to be able to touch us!"

Shane pulled a new cigarette from his pack while he listened to the ghost's rant and then slowly moved himself into his path. August cut his pacing short and stood face to face with Shane.

"People aren't supposed to be able to do that, no," Shane said. He placed the cigarette between his lips and then reached out and laid his hand on August's shoulder. "But some people can do some wild stuff."

August stood dumbfounded, staring at Shane's hand on his shoulder.

"I'll contact you when I learn anything," James confirmed, getting into his car and starting the engine.

Shane walked around to his own car and tossed the small box containing August's silver coin into his passenger seat. The ghost watched him with an unreadable expression.

"You're like the woman," he said at last.

"Maybe," Shane said. "I don't know who she is, but I don't think it matters much."

"Have you ever..." August didn't finish his question. Behind him, James had pulled out and turned his car. He drove to the end of the driveway and left the property.

"Killed a ghost?" Shane finished.

August said nothing.

"I wouldn't call it that. You're not alive. So you can't be killed. But yeah. I have destroyed some."

He could see August tense and wondered if it would be a recurring thing with him. He didn't expect every spirit he met to be brave and bold, but August's timidity and lack of confidence were already wearing a bit thin.

"Listen, you don't know me, and I don't know you. I trust James, though, and he wants to help you," Shane said. "What you told me sounds serious, so I'll go check it out if you want. But if you don't, let me know. I'll send you back to James or drop your coin off wherever works for you, and that can be it."

August was quiet for long enough that Shane felt his impatience growing. Finally, the ghost took a step forward and then stopped again.

"I want to trust you," he said finally. "I want your help. I'm just... scared, I guess. Maybe that sounds dumb. I'm scared of dying again."

The sentiment was not something Shane had heard from many ghosts. He had never stopped to consider the feelings of most of the ghosts he had destroyed over the years. If he was doing it, it was because they had asked for it in one way or another.

"My business partner did this," August continued, pointing at the broken side of his head. "We were supposed to open a restaurant, and the money kept going out but nothing was coming in. I had contractors and suppliers demanding money I knew I'd already paid. He was taking it all... and when I confronted him, he smashed my head on the edge of a marble countertop. He didn't even say anything. Then he just left me there. Can you believe that?"

"Some people approach murder a little more harshly than others," Shane said.

"It hurt. It hurt a lot," the ghost said. "It took a long time to die. But I was alone, it was late, and no one else was around. I remember dying so clearly. The whole process was so lonely and cold, and I can't do it again. For an hour or a second, I don't want to experience it again."

Shane took another long puff on his cigarette and then exhaled with a shrug.

"I get it. As much as I can while still being alive. You're not the first dead guy to have not enjoyed his death. I'm not looking to hurt you, if that's what you're worried about. You saw the ghosts in my house. I'm just like your Mr. Winston. Only difference is I can touch spirits. Destroy them. But if you want to stop the people who almost did you in, and took out your friends, I'm going to need your help."

August nodded, weakly at first and then more emphatically as though he had convinced himself to agree with Shane.

"Yeah. Yes, okay. I can do that."

"Good. Get in the car."

Shane got in the driver's seat and started the car, not waiting for the ghost. The engine rumbled, and he put it in gear as the ghost manifested on the passenger seat, on top of the box that held his silver coin.

"Honestly, I'm less worried about the people than the ghost in the box," August said as Shane hit the road, heading toward Manchester. He hadn't been to the city in a while, but it was barely a half-hour away.

"What's with you and this box? You have no idea what's in it, you just heard it was a deadly ghost. You don't really know, right?" Shane asked.

"It's not," August said. "I didn't want to tell Mr. Moran, but I know who it is. I know the ghost in the box."

Shane pulled off Berkley Street and took a right turn, glancing briefly at the ghost.

"Who was it?" he asked.

August kept his eyes forward. He sat with his hands on his lap like a child and just watched the road and oncoming traffic while he spoke.

"His name is Cassius. I think he came from the eighteen hundreds, I don't know for sure. Mr. Winston bought him thinking he was something else. He was tricked."

"What did he think he was getting?" Shane asked.

The question made August even more nervous, and it was clear that he was uncomfortable discussing the topic. The fact that he hadn't wanted to include James Moran was also suspicious.

"Mr. Winston was a lonely man. But he was truly a good soul. He cared about other people. He'd ask me about my life and my training every time we cooked. He was always interested in everything I had to say. It was the same with the others. He had a big heart."

"Okay," Shane said.

There was a sense that August was building to something he didn't want to say. He'd only known the ghost for a couple of hours, but Shane could see that he was not used to broaching uncomfortable subjects. Maybe it was their lack of familiarity, or maybe August had always been like that. Either way, he needed to get over it if he wanted Shane to understand anything he was telling him.

"He chose me because I cooked. And Otani played chess. Mitchell played piano. Silva was an actor. We all offered something he valued. The box was supposed to be a more… intimate companion."

Shane paused at a red light, smoke rising in a thin wisp from his cigarette. He raised an eyebrow and waited for the ghost to continue, but he did not.

"He tried to buy a ghost… lover?" Shane said, struggling briefly for a suitable word.

"It sounds crass. The financial transaction is just how these things work. He bought my coin, but he didn't buy me," August said defensively.

"Sure," Shane agreed.

"He wanted a wife. He never had a girlfriend, he said he was never comfortable with women, never able to be himself. He was a young man at this time, remember. Just awkward with women and aware of this other world, a world of spirits. He had searched for a ghost, someone who would never have to grow old or distant."

"Someone he could keep in a box," Shane added.

August scowled.

"He wasn't like that," he protested. "He found what he thought was the right person. I'm not sure how much he paid, but I know it was a considerable sum. Mr. Winston was well off, but he was not obscenely rich. He invested a lot in that spirit. And it turned out to be a fraud."

"So he tried to buy a wife and got a killer instead?"

"He did," August replied. "The seller would not take it back. He called

34

it Mr. Winston's burden. Told him to throw it away if he didn't want it, but there would be no refund. And, of course, there was no legal recourse in a case like this. He couldn't sue for fraudulent ghost."

"No, I imagine not," Shane said. "But why not get rid of it? He could have dropped it in the ocean or buried it in a hole where no one would ever find it."

"He couldn't have lived with that. The guilt would have consumed him. Fear it would break free or be found. After he learned what it was, he had to keep it hidden."

Shane grunted and switched lanes, checking the road signs to see where his next turn might be.

"So why keep it from James?"

"I don't know where Mr. Winston procured the spirit. It was long ago, before Mr. Moran's time, I'm sure, but I have heard that Mr. Moran's family has sold haunted items for generations. I feared maybe it was something his family had been involved in or, at the least, an associate."

"And you still wanted to get his help, so you didn't want to alienate him," Shane said.

"It wasn't like that," August replied with little conviction.

Shane grinned, taking a turn and shaking his head.

"You can be honest; I won't hold it against you. You made a desperate play by sending yourself to him, and you played your cards close to your chest because you didn't know if you could trust him, you just didn't have a choice."

August laughed, the first time he showed any sign of levity since their meeting.

"Am I that transparent?"

"You're a ghost," Shane replied. "Transparency is what you do best."

They were on the Everett Turnpike to Manchester. Shane finished his cigarette. He glanced at August again.

"So, Winston gets scammed on a ghost wife and ends up with a box

35

that housed a murderer. When do you think this happened?"

"Around fifty years ago, sixty maybe?"

"So this was an in-person deal, then. No internet, no brokers. He tracked this seller down, made the purchase, and got scammed. They must have swapped the real ghost for the fake one at the last minute," Shane said.

"Probably," August agreed. "It was years later when I came to be part of his home, so I only know the little bits I heard. I could be significantly off on the years, but that was my understanding."

"Doesn't matter. Point is, it was a while ago. And he kept this under wraps pretty well. So much that even you, in his house, barely knew about it."

"None of us did."

"So who did? Who told these Harvesters about what was in the box?"

If what August said was true, Winston was not likely to be bragging about his murder box out in the open. It sounded more like a secret burden he planned to take to the grave. The only other person who would have known was the scammer, someone who had supplied it to him maybe sixty years ago. Why would anyone sit on that for sixty years and then sell the information to a group of hunters?

"I don't know," August answered. Shane hadn't expected him to. It was a question he'd have to ask the Harvesters when he found them.

Assuming everyone stayed alive long enough to talk.

CHAPTER 5
AMONG THE DEAD

August easily guided Shane to the house once they were back within Manchester city limits. As Shane had learned, August and Winston frequently went shopping together and sometimes visited restaurants. According to the ghost, Winston took him discreetly into a restaurant and if no one reacted as though they could see him, the man ordered a meal and August snuck into the kitchen to see how it was made so he could recreate it later.

Winston lived on the edge of the town, not far from where open countryside, golf courses, and an industrial area took over. Although he was in a residential area with neighbors on both sides, he had a large property that offered a decent amount of privacy for his ghostly companions.

Shane drove by the house once without slowing to get a feel for the neighborhood and observe everything in it. The front driveway was empty, and the house looked unremarkable from the outside. There was no sign anything horrible had happened there recently, and if it had been processed as a crime scene, there was no indication of it.

August did not see any signs of the Harvesters, either. He didn't recognize any vehicles that were parked nearby, and nothing stood out in his mind.

"Everything looks fine," he said. "Same as always."

Shane circled the block and came back a second time so the ghost could have another look in case there was something he missed.

"You said before that the Harvesters came back when you came back.

Where did they come from?" Shane asked.

"I'm not sure, but they were fast. They couldn't have been too far away."

"And you don't see any unusual vehicles now? Nothing out of place?"

"Not that I can think of. I didn't spend much time looking at the neighbor's cars."

It seemed unlikely that the ghost would recognize anything worth his attention on another pass. Shane slowed his car and parked on the street a short distance from Winston's house. If there was a dead body inside, he didn't want his to be the last car anyone saw parked out front.

"What do we do now?" August said.

"Go have a look inside,"

August looked out the window and then back at Shane.

"Just through the door?"

"Unless there's a better way. If you look like you know where you're going, most people won't look at you twice. I assume the door's unlocked, so I'll just head in. No one bats an eye."

"Mr. Winston could still be in there."

"He probably is," Shane agreed. "Won't be the first dead body I've seen."

He leaned past the ghost and opened the glove box, pulling out a pair of gloves and slipping them on. He tucked the box with the coin inside then closed it before leaning back and opening his door.

"You ready?"

"Not really," the ghost answered. Shane ignored him and got out of the car. He headed down the sidewalk at a casual pace and then turned up the driveway. August had not joined him, but Shane wasn't worried about the ghost. He just needed to get into the house.

The gloves would ensure he didn't leave fingerprints at a potential crime scene. He didn't need to be caught up in another murder investigation. He didn't have the time or patience for it.

Winston's front door was unlocked as Shane had suspected. He pushed it casually and strode into the house like it was his own. The smell hit him in the face so hard he nearly stopped, but he continued forward, not wanting to look suspicious to anyone who might be glancing in his direction.

Someone had definitely died in the house. The smell was unmistakable. Winston had been dead for days and the house was warm, making the decay worse.

The curtains were drawn and there were no lights on, but it was still bright enough to see that flies were swarming as Shane made his way to the living room.

Winston's body was laid out on the floor face-down. Insects were hard at work feasting and breeding on the body. The surrounding carpet was stained brown for nearly a foot in all directions. It stood in stark contrast to what was otherwise a pristine and well-maintained home, like a shocking vulgarity in a place it was never meant to be.

Shane could see the bullet wound that had taken the man's life. With the rate of decay, thanks to the temperature and the insects, it would likely not be visible much longer.

"Oh."

August had entered the room from the wall to Shane's left. He stood there, just a couple of paces from the body on the floor, staring at it blankly. From what August had told Shane, he had rushed out of the house soon after Winston had died. There had been little time for him to inspect the body or come to terms with what had happened.

Shane understood that there was a vast difference between knowing someone was dead and seeing their body. The condition Winston was in did August no favors. Ghost or not, very few people could accept the sight of a dead person in such a state without feeling horror and revulsion.

"Does that happen to everyone when they die?" August asked.

"Depends on how you die, I suppose," Shane said.

A person could die in a million ways, and a million things could happen to the body after that. There weren't a lot of especially pleasant ways to die, but there were certainly more gruesome ones than others. If a body was left in the open, then the ravages of time were quick and brutal.

August lifted his hand slowly and touched the wound on the side of his head. His eyes were locked on his friend's corpse. Shane knew some spirits visited their bodies after death.

Eloise and Carl still spent time with their remains, and each had endured the process of watching their bodies rot away within the walls of the house on Berkley Street. But those deaths weren't the same as this. Very few insects invaded the house to consume their bodies, for one.

"Just food in the end, huh?" the ghost said softly. "Just meat."

"That's all the body is," Shane agreed. "Meat. A person is another thing altogether."

"We can't leave him like this," August said. "It's not right."

The ghost got down on his knees, leaning over the body of his dead friend. The smell, the stains on the floor, and the maggots didn't affect him. He could neither smell nor feel any of it. All August saw was someone that he cared about who had been murdered and left behind like garbage.

He reached out his hand and laid it on the dead man's head. Flies buzzed away, disturbed by the rush of cold air that the ghost brought with him. They didn't move far, and they were barely disturbed, but the action still cleared a small space.

"He was my friend," August said.

"We'll make sure he's taken care of. But not yet. We have to be smart about this," Shane reminded him.

August was silent for a long moment before finally nodding and getting back to his feet. He looked at his hand to check if it had the congealed blood of his friend, but there was nothing. Still, he rubbed his hands together as though cleaning them and then wiped them on his pants.

Shane left the room and ventured deeper into the house. Little looked like it had been disturbed, and it was clear the Harvesters had not robbed the house or otherwise made a mess of things.

He made his way to the bedroom and saw the exposed wall safe with its door still open. There were some documents inside but nothing else. August joined Shane a moment later and pointed it out to him, even though he was already inspecting it.

"That's where the box was," he explained.

Below the safe was a small shelving unit that looked much rougher. Books and some other knickknacks had been torn apart. The wood was cracked and broken, and it looked like someone had taken a sledgehammer to the top two shelves.

"They hit this thing hard," Shane said.

"It was where the other items were. Silva and Otani and Mitchell. Sometimes, Mr. Winston would leave everyone sitting out like that," August explained.

Now that Shane knew what had been on the shelf, it made sense. Haunted objects could not endure their ghosts being destroyed. The shared energy damaged both when the end came.

"But they took the broken items?" Shane said.

August looked over the junk on the floor and nodded.

"All three," he said.

Most collectors wanted a haunted item because of the ghost that was bound to it. It seemed like the Harvesters wanted the opposite. They wanted the destroyed item to prove that the ghost had been vanquished. Like taking the horn from a rhino, or the tusks from an elephant. It was a ruined trophy to prove their win.

They left the bedroom and continued toward the rear of the house. Shane paused when they reached the kitchen, his attention focused on several empty soda cans on the counter next to the sink. He approached them, lifting each one and shaking it to see how much was left. Aside from a dribble in the bottom, they were empty.

Nearby, a half-pot of coffee was still in a coffee maker. Shane touched the glass, and it was still warm.

"Winston kept the house clean?" Shane asked.

"Spotless. He was very thorough," August said.

"Not a guy to leave cans on the counter?"

He held one up, and the ghost looked at it and shook his head.

"No, he wasn't."

"They've been back," Shane said.

"I told you, they went back the next day."

"No. More recent." Shane nodded toward the coffee pot.

Despite the smell, the Harvesters continued to visit Winston's home.

"They're still looking for me?"

"Or, your man, Cassius, must still be on the loose," Shane said.

He could think of nothing else that made sense. If they set the ghost free like what August said, then they must have still been looking for it. And if they were using Winston's house as the base of operations even with his corpse rotting in the living room, then the box couldn't have gone far. It was the central location at which they regrouped.

"Still?" August said, the worry plain in his voice.

"Unless they like the ambiance of their murder scene, I'd say so. They're persistent and a bit reckless in how they work. Makes them more dangerous than they already are."

"So, what can we do?" the ghost asked.

"We hunt."

CHAPTER 6

JOINING THE HUNT

Shane stood in the yard behind Winston's house. The rear of the property was much larger than he expected and opened out into a field and some train tracks in the distance. The property was lined with trees, and it had a very woodsy feel to it, even though it was still in the city.

There was a gate at the back of the property that led from Winston's yard into the open field. The gate was open, and the long, uncut grass around it was tamped down.

"They headed that way," Shane said, pointing into the field. It looked like several people had been through and had stomped down a path from the house toward the railroad tracks.

"That's all industrial back there," August said, indicating the featureless buildings beyond the tracks.

It looked like a series of warehouses or factories, nothing with any discernible name on the wall that Shane could see from where they were. Some had heavy equipment parked in their lots, forklifts, transport trucks, and piles of wooden pallets or plastic cases.

"Any idea what kind of businesses?" Shane asked.

"Mostly food. There's a bottling plant. The one right ahead does frozen fish. Frozen vegetables and fruits over there. I think one is frozen pizza."

"Lots of cold storage then," Shane said.

"Most of the workers have to bundle up from what I've seen. Probably very cold," August agreed.

Shane nodded and followed the path of flattened grass toward the buildings. August came with him as he trudged onward, following the path that had been left for them by whoever had gone through Winston's property.

"Why would they go this way?" August asked.

"Cold," Shane said. "You said they had gear with them, mentioned something about heat sinks."

"One of them said something like that," August confirmed.

"That's how they track you. Thermal scans. Ghosts don't have body heat; they suck it up. That's why you're so cold. Thermal images can show you a living target, but also dead. They'll register as well below ambient."

"So won't these factories make their tools useless?"

"You bet. I'm guessing Cassius figured that out. If I were a ghost being hunted with thermal trackers, that's where I'd hide."

They reached the railroad tracks and Shane stopped, standing on a pile of track ballast at the edge of the raised surface on which four sets of tracks seemed to run forever in both directions. He could see no one moving, living or dead.

Shane quickly crossed the tracks and then ducked low behind the fence of the plant that August said made frozen pizzas. Ivy and other weeds covered it near the ground, and the metal was rusty from years of neglect. It looked like anyone even approaching the fence was a rare occurrence.

The rear lot behind the plant was made of cracked and uneven pavement. There were rusted, old racks, some pieces of forgotten industrial machinery, and a lot of weeds. Closer to the building was a small section used for parking with maybe two dozen cars present.

He could see mounted lights and security cameras on the walls, but most were trained around the doors and the entrance to the lot on the far right side.

"How long are they going to hunt him like this?" August asked. "People are working here. How would they even get in?"

"Like I said, if you act like you belong somewhere, most people won't bat an eye."

"In a frozen food processing plant?" the ghost countered.

"It's not an army base or a bank vault. Who cares if someone's walking around inside a pizza factory?"

"But the ghost could hurt them or the innocent people inside."

Shane felt like giving August a shake because he still wasn't appreciating the full spectrum of the issue. These people had shot his friend in the head for being in their way. They didn't care if a ghost hurt innocent people in a frozen food plant.

"It could. That's why we need to be careful. Of Cassius and these Harvesters. The upside is, no one is expecting me, so I'll be just another face in the crowd."

"And me? They'll recognize me."

"Then you need to stay off their radar until I get the upper hand," Shane explained. "You can move in shadows, can't you?"

"You mean walk around in the dark?" August asked.

Shane sighed. If it wasn't for the naked sincerity that the ghost exuded, he would have been certain he was playing a joke.

"Hide in shadows. Fade into walls. Be the dark. You know, stuff ghosts do."

"Oh," August replied.

There was no immediate follow-up, and Shane shook his head and grabbed the fence.

"Stay out of sight but keep an eye out for these Harvesters. Let me know if you see any."

Shane climbed the fence quickly, hopped down into the lot behind the frozen food plant, removed his gloves so as not to look conspicuous, and made a beeline for the door off the parking lot. He didn't hide or duck away from any cameras; he just wanted to look like anyone else heading into work.

August crept past the fence and darted from shadow to shadow, and Shane ignored it. At least he wouldn't show up on camera. That was some small saving grace.

Shane reached the door to the plant and headed inside. The interior was a narrow hallway that led straight and left. The floors were covered in ugly brown tile, and the walls were cream-colored and in desperate need of cleaning. Shane continued forward to a large set of double doors and let himself onto the manufacturing floor.

The interior of the plant was massive and extremely cold. The thrum of machines was nearly deafening as belts, motors, and more whirred and hummed and rattled along.

Before him, a line of workers hand-topped cheese-covered dough at a rapid pace as it ran unceasingly down a conveyor belt to some kind of machine. On the far side, he saw another machine wrapping the dough in plastic and sealing it with a bead of heat.

Everyone working the line wore hair nets and gloves along with what looked like lightweight white coveralls. Shane cursed silently but started moving immediately, making it look like he had a reason to be there.

He walked the exterior of the room, looking at everyone he passed. No one stood out right away as someone who didn't belong, and there was no sign of a ghost.

Shane reached the end of the line and the doors to the industrial-sized freezers where workers were packing the boxed pizzas for transport. August joined him from behind a cooling unit.

"I don't see anyone yet."

"Neither do I," Shane said. "If the ghost is here, he's lying low."

He circled to the far side and had already caught the attention of at least one employee who kept looking in his direction. Shane ignored the man, refusing to make eye contact and instead inspecting the facility as though he knew what the machines were and was just interested in ensuring they were working correctly.

They made it halfway across the plant before August ducked behind a bank of machines and dropped to the ground, his eyes wide with panic.

"What?" Shane asked casually as though nothing was out of the ordinary.

"There's a thin man with glasses ahead of us, dressed like a worker. He has a device in his hands. He's one of them," the ghost said.

Shane glanced around the room and saw who August meant. The man stood a short distance from a group of workers visually inspecting the pizzas and pulling out inconsistent ones. Shane could not see what he was doing, but he held a tablet that had some sort of sensor mounted on the back.

The Harvester continued to check his gear as he slowly moved around and pointed the tablet in different directions. If he was scanning for a ghost using a thermal imager, it wouldn't have been working, given the low temperature in the plant. The man seemed otherwise unobtrusive, and no one gave him a second glance. Even when Shane followed him to the farthest edge of the plant, he didn't engage in any attention-drawing behavior.

Shane was not quite as lucky as the Harvester. The employee who had been looking at him earlier had returned, making a beeline across the factory toward Shane. August had vanished. Not wanting to look suspicious, Shane waited for the man to approach.

"Excuse me, sir?" the employee said to Shane. "Who are you?"

"Hi," Shane replied, smiling at the man in white coveralls. "My name's Paul. I was here looking into applying for a job, but I don't know where to go."

The man in the coveralls grimaced, looking exasperated, and held his arm out to shepherd Shane away from the production floor.

"Okay, well, this is not the place to do it. We don't just take walk-ins. You need to email your resume to the office, and when we're hiring, if you're on file, we'll reach out to you."

"I just figured it'd be easier to walk in and shake someone's hand, you know?" Shane said.

"Unfortunately, it doesn't work that way, and I'm going to need you to leave. We have hygiene standards that need to be upheld, and you're just here in street clothes."

Shane went without any fuss, letting the man usher him toward the door, agreeing with everything the man said and appearing at least vaguely apologetic for causing any trouble.

"So, email, then?" he asked as the man took him to the exit.

"Absolutely. Go to the website and follow the instructions there."

"Sure, sure, great," Shane replied. "But this is a good place to work, right? I heard there was some trouble over the past few days."

The man looked perplexed and shook his head.

"I don't know who said that, but I doubt it was anyone working here. Everything's been fine. We have strict protocols here, and no safety issues, accidents, or trouble. Now please, sir, I need you to head out. Apply online. That's how we do it."

"Sure thing, yeah." Shane smiled before turning away and leaving.

If the ghost or the Harvesters had caused any trouble, the man would have known about it. He seemed like a floor supervisor, but his reaction was sincere from what Shane could see. Nothing had happened in the plant since Winston had died. The ghost they were looking for was not here.

The fact that there was a Harvester on site meant that they didn't know where the ghost was, either. Shane guessed he would find similar people at the other plants nearby if he went looking.

While the factories seemed like the most likely places for a ghost to hide, it was still a proverbial needle in the haystack. There were a handful of processing plants to choose from. Finding the ghost would take some time unless he found a way to narrow the search parameters.

Shane exited the building into the parking lot and then took a left off the property through the gate, rather than hopping the fence back toward the train tracks. He headed out onto the street and then started walking along a cracked and poorly kept road toward the next facility.

August appeared once Shane had passed a series of trucks in front of the next plant. The ghost looked nervous and swept his head in all directions as they moved as though he feared an ambush even though there were few places from which anyone could get the drop on them.

"That was close," he said.

Shane lit a cigarette and laughed, exhaling smoke at him.

"In what way?"

"That man. He caught you. He knew you didn't belong."

"Yeah, he did," Shane agreed, waiting for the ghost to continue.

"So, what if he called the police? Or the Harvesters saw? Or Cassius?"

Shane shook his head.

"You're a weird guy, August," he said. "You've seriously never been in a fight?"

"What does that have to do with anything?"

"Just curious. You've never killed anyone?"

"God, no," the ghost replied.

"Hit anyone? Living or dead?"

The ghost shook his head again.

"I told you no already. I was bullied as a boy. And obviously, I lost a fight," he said, pointing to his head wound. "But I never engaged in any kind of combat."

Shane laughed again.

"Okay, just take it down a notch. A guy who works in a factory saw me and asked me to leave. That's not a threat to my life. If a Harvester saw me, he would have seen a guy being asked to leave. If Cassius saw me, he would have seen a guy being asked to leave. I'm no one. There was no fight, no threat, and no reason for any feathers to get ruffled. That went pretty much exactly as I planned."

"But what if they called someone? Held you for trespassing?"

"The real world is not on the brink of destruction at every moment. People don't care. If you work with them, they work with you. If I'm not making trouble, they won't make trouble. That's how you get things done smoothly. When I need to make trouble, you'll know. And when that happens, you can't let fear freeze you up. If we get into a scrape, you may need to hold your own out there."

"You need me to fight?"

He sounded appalled as much as he was surprised. Shane exhaled smoke again.

"I don't need you to, but if you see an opportunity, it might help. And anyway, don't you want revenge for your friend?"

"I'm not a fighter. I don't even know how to throw a punch."

"You're dead, though. Doesn't matter if you know how to fight. You can put your hand into someone's chest and crush their heart."

"Oh my God," the ghost said, offended at the suggestion.

"Something to think about. If I'm in a position where I'm about to die and you can save me by ripping out someone's heart, know that I support and encourage the action. But, you know, if you don't want to get involved, I'm not expecting it. Just don't get in the way. And avoid this woman who can destroy ghosts."

"I never want to see her again in my life," August said.

Shane could only laugh again. The ghost wasn't alive, his wish had already been granted.

CHAPTER 7

IN THE COLD

August did his best to stay out of sight as they headed to the next facility. Shane repeated the procedure from the first one but was caught much more quickly this time by a diligent supervisor who recognized that Shane didn't belong on the floor. It didn't matter either way as there was no sign of the ghost having been there, either.

It didn't look like there were any Harvesters in that plant, but Shane didn't have enough time to inspect it fully. August was not willing to stay around to keep an eye on things without Shane.

They headed to the frozen vegetable processing facility next that was much larger and less organized. No one stopped Shane; no one even looked in his direction more than once. He did a thorough sweep of the building and even ventured into the large freezers, which had the lowest temperatures and would have been ideal for hiding. There was nothing.

Time was slipping away. Shane intended to look through every facility that he could access, but he suspected it would get harder if the plants closed at the end of the workday. He wasn't sure if they ran twenty-four-hour shifts, and he didn't want to have to trespass instead of just looking like a lost person wandering where he shouldn't be.

The last facility on the same side of the street closest to the train tracks was Ocean Imperial Fish. Shane recognized the logo on the outside of the building from boxes of fish sticks he'd seen in stores over the years. The plant was massive, dwarfing the others they'd searched.

"Who knew fish sticks were so popular?" he said as they approached the entrance.

Despite the size of the plant, there was a suspicious lack of activity outside. The large parking lot that came off the main road was empty of all but three passenger vehicles and a row of parked trailers. No sound came from the inside, while all the others had the dull mechanical hum of machines in the background.

A pair of locked glass doors barred the entrance. Shane lifted his hands to shield his eyes and pressed his face to the window to look inside. A security guard seated at a desk stared back at him and then got to his feet, walking slowly to the door and pulling on a keychain to find the right key to unlock it.

"Can I help you?" the guard asked, standing in the doorway.

He was an older man, but he was solidly built. He looked like he might have been a fighter thirty years ago and still cut an intimidating figure.

"Hey, yeah. I just got into town, and I was looking for my brother. He works here, but I guess... you're not open?" Shane said.

"Closed today. Had a serious accident yesterday, and everyone is off until things are cleaned up."

"Oh wow, what happened? I haven't talked to my brother since a few days ago. I hope he's okay," Shane said, sounding concerned.

The guard's expression became sympathetic but awkward.

"Yeah, you'll need to talk to someone in management about that. I mean, I'm not supposed to talk to anyone, but... there was an issue with the cryogenic freezers. Some nitrogen tanks blew, and a few workers died. If I were you, I'd get in touch with your family just to make sure."

"Oh no," Shane said. "What caused the accident? Aren't there ways to prevent that sort of thing?"

"Usually," the guard replied. "Had guys in here all day looking into it to figure it out. It's like they just burst for no reason. Going to lead to some big lawsuits, I can tell you that."

The guard suddenly seemed to realize he was speaking out of turn and cleared his throat.

"Anyway, I'd recommend calling your brother or the company's main line," he said before checking his watch. "During business hours."

"Of course. Thank you," Shane replied, walking away.

The guard locked the door behind him and returned to his desk. Shane glanced at the camera placement as he got out of sight of the building.

He ducked behind the row of parked trailers and waited for August to reappear.

"You catch all that?" Shane asked.

"I did. The timing seems a little suspicious."

"It certainly does," Shane agreed. "Nitrogen tanks bursting and killing people is a hell of an accident to happen out of the blue. This is our spot."

"How can you be sure?" the ghost asked.

"I can't. Not until you go have a look around inside."

August shook his head, looking past the trailers to the plant.

"If they catch me, I'm done for."

"They're not here yet. If they were, that guard would be dead now. But the ghost might still be here. That's who you need to look for."

"If he sees me, he could come for me, too."

"Maybe," Shane said. "But since he doesn't know you from a hole in the ground, he probably won't care if another ghost passes through. And even if he does, just run away. I doubt he'd risk following."

"A lot of the things you say are just based on your opinions; did you know that?" August asked.

"My opinions are based on a lot of experience. Yours?"

Shane didn't want to waste any more time to give August a pep talk. They had spent hours searching the other facilities, and the sooner they could track down Cassius, the sooner August would get the results he hoped for. Shane could have done it all, but it would take more time and would be riskier. Things would be so much easier if August was just willing to stick his neck out a little bit.

"This was your idea," Shane went on. "You wanted to find this ghost and stop him."

"Fine," the ghost said. "I'll go"

"Stay out of sight and you'll be fine. Remember, you can run if you need to and go places the living can't."

"Yeah, I have the advantage," August said, more to himself than to Shane.

The ghost returned his focus to the plant and genuinely looked like he was ready to take the initiative and head out. He didn't make it more than a step before he stopped and ducked.

"What now?" Shane asked.

"There," the ghost replied.

His attention was on the far side of the street, in a parking lot opposite the frozen fish plant. A handful of cars were in a tree-lined lot next to a dark office building. Shane looked but could see nothing out of the ordinary at first.

"It's the black one, next to the small red car," August said.

Shane saw what the ghost was referring to, a black SUV with dark windows.

"That's one of theirs."

Shane squinted to focus. He thought he could see two figures through the windshield, but it was hard to tell. If they were parked across the street scouting the building, they might have seen him when he approached. His conversation with the security guard might have roused their suspicions, but when he left without incident, he figured they would not have paid him another glance.

August had walked with him part of the way to the trucks where they were currently hiding, but he couldn't recall if the ghost had been well-hidden. He had traveled in the shadows as Shane had instructed, but Shane had also given up on the ghost's abilities some time ago.

"They would have come by now if they'd seen you," Shane said. "They're probably not using thermal scans from there. These guys are just on a stakeout."

"So, they know the ghost is here," August said.

"They think he is. But they can't get access without alerting security. This place has probably been under serious scrutiny since yesterday. Probably had cops and emergency crews all over. They don't want the heat off that."

"So, what's the plan?"

"They're waiting for their shot. Nighttime will be best. We're going to do the same."

"But then we'll get caught," August complained.

"Maybe. We'll circle out of view of these two. There might be more in the back, but we'll be better able to deal with them if they're isolated. We take out the security cameras and sneak in through a rear door. With any luck, we can be in and out before they make their move."

"And if we aren't lucky?"

"Then we fight," Shane said.

He turned on the ghost and took him by the shoulders, staring him in the eyes. August was uncomfortable and tried to shrink away, but Shane held him fast.

"Sooner or later, this is going to get ugly. I need you to accept that and be ready to do something about it or make sure you are out of my way."

"I know," August said, shrugging Shane off. "I heard you the first time."

"I don't need you to just hear it, I need you to understand. Do you understand me?"

"Yes," the ghost answered.

"Good. James is going to owe me for this one."

Shane stuck to the far side of the trucks and made his way around to the side of the building. From where the Harvesters were parked across the street, they had a poor eyeline to Shane's location, but he still stayed down and out of the way as they passed the side of the plant and headed to the rear.

Behind the facility were loading docks, dumpsters, and some equipment storage. It was tidier than the pizza plant, and someone was earning their paycheck making sure weeds weren't growing over the fence and filling the lot.

None of the equipment looked familiar to Shane, but they offered a good place to keep out of sight of security, cameras, or the Harvesters.

"Doesn't look like anyone's back here," August said.

"Some cameras though," Shane said. "We'll wait a bit, and then I'm going to need you to knock them out so I can get in."

"How do I do that?" August asked. He was crouched with Shane next to some bulky machine part.

"You literally knock them out of the way. Strip the wires if you're feeling adventurous; I don't care."

"Okay," August said with determination.

They kept an eye on the plant from the back until the sun began its slow descent in the west. The other facilities that weren't running on twenty-four-hour schedules had already let out, and there was significantly less traffic on the street as a result. Things were quieter, even though the daylight had barely diminished.

"We should make a move now," Shane suggested. "Before the Harvesters do."

"Okay, good. Yes. I'll just move the cameras," August agreed.

The ghost took a moment to psych himself up for the event and then ran from his hiding place to the nearest camera. Shane let him work at his own pace, hoping that the result would still be something useful.

If nothing else, August proved adept at following instructions. The ghost started up the walls like a spider and forced the cameras upward. He disappeared into the wall after, in an uncharacteristic display of initiative that surprised Shane.

Several minutes passed before the ghost emerged and darted back across the lot toward where Shane was hidden.

"That was good," Shane said, but the ghost shook his head.

"I think they're here," he replied.

"The Harvesters?"

"Yes. I was going to disable the cameras inside by the door, but they weren't working. It looks like someone turned off their power."

Shane cursed. He expected to be getting the jump on them, but he had underestimated their eagerness. The longer he waited around outside, now, the more opportunity they would have to catch up with Cassius and then be on their way.

"What should we do?" August asked. "Wait for them to leave?"

Shane scoffed and made his way to the door.

"No. We get Cassius before they do and put them out of business in the process."

CHAPTER 8
SPILLING BLOOD

The interior of the plant was freezing. The door clicked louder than Shane would have liked and, because the space was empty, it echoed through the facility. He could do nothing but move swiftly away from it in case the sound had drawn attention.

Ocean Imperial Fish was impossibly large inside. The production floor was a vast network of conveyor belts and machinery that Shane had never seen and couldn't even guess the purpose of. Without people manning the equipment, it all looked like a strange, mechanical Stonehenge.

There were enormous industrial freezers inside the building, and one was turned off and empty. It must have been the one that suffered the nitrogen tank accident that cost several employees their lives. Shane had a feeling it was the result of this ghost, Cassius.

August stayed by Shane's side as they made their way to the damaged freezer. He could see where a section had been cordoned off, and that everything housed in the freezer was removed.

Only several minutes had passed when a noise from the far side of the plant caught Shane's attention. It was a bang, like someone had closed a thin, metal door.

"What was that?" August whispered. Shane waved him to silence and kept listening, but there was no follow-up.

Quickly, and as quietly as possible, Shane made his way across the facility. He kept low to the ground and paused every few yards to listen again in case there were any new sounds, drawing closer to what he thought was the origin of the noise.

"Where do you think you're going?"

The strange voice echoed across the empty plant. It was hard for Shane to pinpoint the origin, save for realizing it came from somewhere ahead of them among the machines. It was a man's voice, not very old, and with no discernible accent.

Shane paused, crouched next to the control panel for a conveyor belt. He could see nothing ahead or behind him, and to his right was an empty wall. It seemed an unlikely place for anyone to sneak up on him, but it didn't give him any advantages for getting the drop on someone else, either.

August was crouched with him, half-hidden in the floor. The look on his face was one of panic, and he couldn't even bring himself to speak, which was probably for the best. Nevertheless, Shane raised a finger to his lips to ensure the ghost knew to keep quiet.

"I can see you on the security cameras; there's no sense hiding," the voice yelled.

Shane did not move. If the stranger kept talking to him, he would keep listening. From his hiding place, he could see under the conveyor belts and across the floor in his immediate area. If someone approached, he would be able to see their feet as they moved toward him.

"I'm with building security. If you don't come out now, I'm going to call the police."

"But the cameras don't work," August said in the quietest whisper.

Of course, they don't, Shane thought. His anonymous friend was a Harvester. Also, based on the way he spoke, he was not accustomed to luring people out into the open. Pretending to be building security or threatening to call the police was how you tricked a trespassing teenager. This person may be a professional ghost hunter, but was not a professional at intimidation.

No one was going to call the police, so the Harvesters were likely planning to attack Shane and were trying to keep him busy. August said there were at least five of them, so the fight could have been something more than Shane could handle if they came all at once. His only advantage would be in keeping them at a distance at first and assessing what he was dealing with.

Unhappy with his options, Shane stood.

Across the conveyor belts and approaching from behind a series of sorting machines, five people froze in their tracks.

He looked across the assembled group, taking stock as quickly as he could. There were three men and two women. Two of the men had tablets like Shane had seen earlier. One of them was the man they saw at the pizza plant.

Of the two women, Shane focused on the one at the head of the pack. She was tall with short, blonde hair that was shaved bald on the right side of her head. He saw several piercings and tattoos up her bare, ropey arms. The woman looked muscular, not in a bodybuilder sort of way, but in a way that suggested she could hold her own in a street fight.

Shane had never seen her before, but he knew she was the one who could fight spirits. There was something in the way she carried herself like fear was not something she had time for. The others looked almost like support staff, engineers, or bodyguards or something. They weren't the ones he needed to worry about.

One of the men drew a gun and pointed it in Shane's direction. The woman with the half-shaved head smiled, though just barely.

"You don't look like you're here to get some fish," the man with the gun said.

"No? I love a nice halibut," Shane replied.

The man cocked the hammer of the gun and extended his arm. Shane watched him, saying nothing for several seconds until he noticed the first tremor in the man's arm causing his aim to waver.

"He's a funny guy. I like funny guys," the blonde woman said.

"I'd offer to buy you a drink, but this place doesn't have anything good on tap," Shane replied.

"Who are you?" the man with the gun asked.

The other man with the tablet device was the one Shane had seen earlier in the day, and he was keeping quiet. The third man looked extremely skittish. He was behind the others, and the nervousness couldn't have been plainer on his face. He was the odd man out, and Shane didn't understand what his role was.

The second woman was also farther back, closest to the machine. Shane could see that she was armed, but she hadn't pulled her weapon. The dynamic was not clear, but Shane knew based on what he heard about Winston that they were willing to kill him if they thought he was in the way. The only thing keeping him alive was probably the fact that they didn't know who he was or why he was there.

"Obviously, I'm not security. But, of course, neither are you. And by the looks of it… you're not pulling a frozen fish heist. So, who are you?"

"You're not asking questions, big guy," the gunman said.

"But I just did," Shane shot back.

"Really funny guy," the blonde said, amusement clear in her voice.

Silence fell over the group and Shane waited for someone else to make a move. Instead, something heavy clicked deeper in the facility. The mechanical crunch echoed toward the group as the machine behind the Harvesters buzzed to life.

The conveyor belt ran on rotating, metal rollers toward the sorting machine, which was in a hopper beneath the belt. Metallic drums covered in broad, multi-sized blunt teeth spun rapidly.

The man with the gun turned to see what was happening and before he could say anything, the woman in the back was yanked from her feet. Shane couldn't see the ghost that did it, but he knew it was Cassius. The force of the movement was no accident. The woman had not tripped; she had been thrown.

Shane was already ducking as the woman's scream tore through the plant. He could see the blood spray out of the machine as the gunman dropped his weapon to rescue her.

The blonde woman ignored them all as the others did what they could to save their companion before she was pulled in completely. Instead of focusing on the living, the blonde woman was searching for the ghost.

"Did you see him?" Shane asked August, as he ran from his previous hiding place while the Harvesters were distracted.

"He's behind the machine. He pulled her through it," the ghost told him.

The woman's screams continued while the other Harvesters pulled her body from the machinery and dealt with her wounds. Shane kept looking for Cassius as he circled the room, looking to come at the machinery from behind.

"There!" August said. He stopped moving and pointed ahead.

Shane looked where the ghost had indicated and stopped as well. Cassius was watching his handiwork. He stood in the shadows below a catwalk, muscular arms crossed over a broad chest. In life, he could have easily been a bodybuilder or a professional wrestler.

Cassius was taller than Shane by several inches and definitely would have outweighed him back when he was alive. His face was hidden behind a mane of shaggy, greasy-looking hair that obscured most of his features. He was shirtless, and his body was a patchwork of scars. Some were from knives, but others looked like they might have been from animals. A massive patch of pink, puffy flesh down one side looked like maybe he had been dragged across a road.

As Shane watched, Cassius began to move around the machines. The blonde woman had disappeared, but the ghost was focused on the men. Shane moved to a better vantage point and saw that they had retrieved their companion from the machine. Her legs had been destroyed. She no longer had anything below the knee and was bleeding profusely.

While the others tended to her, the ghost took the man Shane had seen at the pizza plant and hurled him into the next machine in the line. Whatever procedure the machine was meant to perform for frozen fish, it only succeeded in tearing the man apart. Cassius had thrown him in head-first, and there was no chance for the man's survival.

His scream only lasted a second. The sound of bone crunching, wet and loud, hit Shane's ear with an uncomfortable familiarity. The powerful gears were relentless. The device chewed the man's body as though he were made of paper.

The whine of stressed metal rang through the plant. Flesh and bone clogged the gears, straining them beyond their intended use. The motor rumbled and then screeched as it ground to a halt. Blood gushed from the bottom workings of the metal case, and the nervous-looking man screamed loudly and made a run for the exit while the armed man shouted after him to stay where he was.

"Beatrix!" the armed man shouted again.

Before Cassius could make a move on him, the blonde woman appeared from the ghost's opposite side.

She said nothing and instead let her fists do the talking. A right cross to Cassius' jaw landed only a heartbeat before she planted a heel firmly in his kneecap, taking his leg out from under him. Though the ghost was larger than her by far, her attack was designed to use his size against him. She was fleet of foot and showed no hesitation as she hit him twice more and moved away before he had a chance to counter her attack, staying out of range of his huge hands.

The effect of the woman's strikes was more surprising than damaging. The kick to the knee had not crippled him; it merely set him off balance, and he was back on his feet swiftly.

Cassius came for Beatrix, and she dealt him another round of swift jabs and punches. He was ready for her this time, however, and just let her blows rain with no effect. He closed the gap between them and lifted her from the ground by her neck.

Beatrix struggled in his grasp but maintained her composure. She slammed a fist into the ghost's wrist to break free. His hold was like steel, and her attacks didn't even cause his arms to shake.

"Let's see what your insides look like," the ghost said.

CHAPTER 9
THE DEAD MAN

The blonde woman hung like a rag doll in the ghost's grasp. He held her effortlessly, one hand on either side of her thin neck. Shane could see her eyes bulging and her face changing color as the ghost pushed his thumbs against her trachea. He was being slow and methodical, but his plan was clear. He was going to rip her throat apart.

Shane knew what the woman was capable of. He knew she had shot Winston, and she would probably not hesitate to do the same to him if push came to shove. But he knew that only through what August had told him. He wasn't willing to let her die at the hands of a monster like Cassius based on second-hand information. And, in any event, he wanted to take out Cassius himself. Shane could kill her later if he had to.

Focused on Beatrix as he was, the ghost was not alert to Shane rushing up behind him. With his arms raised to hold her, he left his body vulnerable. Shane drove an elbow hard into the ghost's exposed ribs, producing a noticeable crunch.

Cassius groaned between clenched teeth, and his body buckled as his right arm dropped. He released Beatrix and turned to face Shane in time to take a well-timed punch to the nose. Bone broke again, and the ghost stumbled back.

Shane expected the beast to come at him to continue the fight. Instead, the spirit bolted in the opposite direction. As a ghost, he was no longer bound by physics the way a corporeal being was. His size was no limitation, nor were the physical obstacles in his way. He was gone in a flash, and Shane barely saw in which direction he went to.

Beatrix was coughing hoarsely on the ground, rubbing her throat, and taking in oxygen again. Shane passed her without a second glance. She was alive, that was the only favor he would extend her. He wanted to get Cassius before the Harvesters had a chance to regroup.

More of the machinery roared to life throughout the plant. Overhead lighting clicked on, and it seemed like every mechanized thing in the plant was suddenly operating at full power.

"Which way did he go?" August asked.

Shane looked at the ghost and shook his head.

"You didn't see?"

"I thought you were going to fight. I didn't think he'd run off."

"Neither did I."

Shane didn't think for a second that Cassius had fled in fear. This was not an act of cowardice; it was strategy. He doubted the spirit had left the plant. He was likely looking for a way to get the upper hand and finish Shane and the Harvesters off. That meant, as big and brutish as Cassius looked, he wasn't stupid. He was opportunistic. That made him incredibly dangerous.

"He could be anywhere," August said.

"He didn't leave," Shane said, dashing down the length of another belt to a machine that wrapped boxes in plastic.

"How do you know?" August asked.

"Because he's not done killing."

They worked together to search from one end of the plant to the other. As they got closer to where they had left the Harvesters, Shane heard the screams of the woman who had lost her legs. They had kept her alive this long, but it wasn't likely to last. He suspected no one had called an ambulance.

"Help me, please. Beatrix! Lanthimos, please!" the woman cried out.

Her voice was ragged and cracked. She sounded breathless and very clearly in pain. Shane ignored her and kept looking for the ghost. Wherever

Cassius had gone, he was covering his tracks. He kept out of sight, even from August, and he was not looking to bait anyone the way some ghosts would.

"Somebody, please!"

There was a desperate tinge to her voice, the panic that came from someone who knew they were about to die. Shane had heard it in the battlefield before, and he had heard it closer to home as well. Sometimes, it was just misplaced fear. Most times, it wasn't.

"I can't see him anywhere," August whispered.

"Somebody!"

Each scream was fainter. More desperate. Shane could not hear anyone replying. He veered from his search and headed back the way they had come. August seemed unaware that they were changing their search pattern, or he didn't care. In any event, he followed Shane until they were back at the blood-soaked machines.

The body of the man was still protruding from the machine he had jammed. His companions were unconcerned with the remains. Now that he was dead, he was not a priority. The woman was on the floor. Someone had made impromptu tourniquets out of shredded clothing and a belt to tie off her legs. They were doing little to affect the damage. She was immersed in a pool of blood. The fact she was still conscious was remarkable.

"Please," she said, seeing Shane approach, "Call an ambulance. I need... I need a hospital... please."

Shane knelt next to her. Her legs had been severed at the knee and were still bleeding freely despite the tourniquets. There was no hope for a doctor to see her in time. He doubted an ambulance would even show before she had bled out.

"Please," she said again.

"What's your name?" Shane asked.

Her breath was halting, coming in strained gasps. She tried to focus on his face, but the effort of lifting her head proved too much.

"Kraft," she said. "Chloe Kraft."

"Chloe, all right. I'm going to be honest with you, Chloe, it's not looking good."

She choked, and he thought it might have been an attempt at laughter.

"No kidding," she said. "Just… help…"

"Why are we wasting time with her?" August asked. "Cassius could be gone. The rest of the Harvesters, too."

"No one went anywhere," Shane said. "Just keep your eyes open."

He stood up then, among the whirring and droning machines, and looked around the facility.

"Your friend is going to die without your help," he shouted. "You're just going to leave her like this?"

He couldn't say how well the sound traveled given the incessant noise in the plant. He suspected they were close enough to have caught some of it. They wouldn't have bothered to tie off the legs if they were indifferent to her survival. At least one of the three remaining Harvesters gave a damn.

There was no reply. The woman on the floor groaned in pain, and her breathing became shallow. She had minutes left. She was going to die on the floor of a frozen fish plant with a stranger. It was a hell of a way to go.

"You guys want this for yourselves? You okay knowing that if you get taken out, too, you're just going to be abandoned here?"

"Mr. Sensitive," a voice shouted from deeper in the plant. "I'm touched."

It was the other woman yelling out to him, the one called Beatrix.

"If you can't have your team's back, you can't expect them to have yours," Shane yelled back.

He suspected this wasn't an approach that would work on Beatrix. She didn't seem like the kind of woman who would give a damn about pleas to her morality or sense of camaraderie. It wasn't meant for her, though. There were still two others with her. Shane wasn't sure about the armed man, but the one who ran off was impressionable. Maybe he could get him to crack.

"Nice fortune cookie," Beatrix replied. "You could be a youth coach."

Shane chuckled. She was sarcastic and raw. She'd probably seen some things in her time that had jaded her. He could understand. But that didn't mean he would be there to save her again if she fell into the ghost's grasp.

"She's bleeding out."

"Save her yourself if you care so much."

It was the gunman yelling this time, not Beatrix. Shane tried to focus on where the voice came from, but there was too much clutter in his way.

The third man was still missing, and there was no sign of the ghost. Shane hoped that he might draw out the spirit to finish the job with the legless woman. He had failed in luring it.

A gunshot rang out, loud, and remarkably close. August gasped at Shane's side. Shane turned swiftly, surprised by the closeness of it, and found Beatrix standing behind him. She held a gun in her hand, pointed down. Kraft was dead on the floor, a gunshot wound through her head.

They stared at each other. Shane expected her to raise the weapon, but instead, she tucked it into the waistband of her jeans and then crossed her arms over her chest. August had already vanished into the shadows.

"Who the hell are you?" she asked.

The distance between them was not great. Shane could have rushed her before she drew the weapon again. He likely would have overpowered her easily. He saw her attempts to fight Cassius, and while they were admirable, he didn't think she had the power behind her fists to make a difference. Maybe against the unsuspecting dead, but not against him.

"Private contractor," Shane said. "Heard someone's been breaking into the facilities around here."

Beatrix smiled and pulled the gun out again. She aimed at Shane, the barrel pointed low. She was looking for a gut shot. He could have done without that.

"Try again."

"I was hired to find out what happened here the other day. Nitrogen canisters don't just explode and kill people," he said.

Beatrix squeezed the trigger without saying anything. The bullet hit the aluminum edge of the conveyor belts inches from Shane's side.

"I hope you understand that I don't have a lot of time to waste. I've seen you talking to your mousey little ghost friend. I watched you attack the big one. Someone hired you to do what? Hunt him? Or us?"

"No one's paying me," Shane answered. "I'm just looking to clean up a mess and make sure it never happens again."

"The hell does that mean? That some kind of tough-guy code?"

"Means I'm here to make sure people don't keep dying. Looks like that's not a concern of yours."

"It's not," she agreed.

She raised the barrel of the gun and closed the distance between her and Shane. She walked casually and pressed the cold barrel to the side of his head, hard enough that she would leave a bruise if she kept it up.

"Who sent you?"

"No one," he told her. "I heard what happened with Winston, and I came to find this ghost. And you."

"And do what?" she demanded.

Shane looked her in the eye. She was not putting on a front the way a lot of people would have in the situation. Her voice was firm but also dispassionate. She wasn't emotionally invested. If he had to guess, he thought she didn't care how things would turn out. She expected to live, and if everyone else died, it wasn't her concern.

"Stop you."

She smirked, and for a moment, Shane expected her to pull the trigger.

"Who do you work with? The Outfit? Endless Night? Skeleton Crew?"

Shane raised an eyebrow. He wasn't sure if she was listing other

Harvesters, or other groups entirely. He knew the Endless Night, but not the others.

"No one."

"No crew? Come on, smart guy. Where's your team? They set up across the street?"

"I don't hire idiots with computers who get turned into mulch," Shane said, nodding toward the dead man in the machine.

"So, you're just greedy?" she said. "Good money in solo work, huh?"

The tone of her voice was remarkably casual given that she still held a gun to his head. Shane wasn't sure what she expected to hear, so he said nothing.

"Not clamming up on me, are you?" She stood inches from Shane, and he could smell vodka on her along with sweat and blood. He met her gaze once more but still said nothing.

"You know, when you want to get to the meaty part of the clam, there's only one way to do it," she said, leaning in even closer. "You gotta shuck it."

She pulled the trigger, grinning in Shane's face.

CHAPTER 10
RUNNERS

The gun clicked. Nothing happened. Shane realized he was holding his breath and let it go when it was clear he had not been shot. The smile never left Beatrix's face as she pulled the gun from his head and removed the empty clip before replacing it with a fresh one from her back pocket.

"I was hoping I'd get a little scream out of you. No such luck, huh?" she said.

"Maybe next time," Shane said.

"There's not going to be a next time, Solo. This is my hunt. This is my payday. And no one is better at the hunt than me. I don't give a damn who you are or why you're here. I'm doing you a professional courtesy by not splattering your brains across a case of frozen fish sticks. Take it for the gift it is."

"Very gracious of you," Shane replied.

"I am the best, Solo. The goddamn best. Remember it."

She tapped his skull with the barrel of the gun to accentuate her point. Shane debated taking it from her but didn't want to risk it.

"I filed it away, thanks," Shane told her.

"Gotta tell you, though, Solo, you got my curiosity piqued. You want to make it interesting? What, say, we both go after this monster?"

Shane waited for her to say something more. He narrowed his eyes when she had no further thoughts to share.

"You mean a bet?" he asked.

"Handsome and smart. You're the total package, I see. What do you say? We both go for the ghost. Winner gets to live."

Before Shane could offer some choice words on her bet, the sound of a siren in the distance drew his attention. He paused to listen, and Beatrix did the same. It was growing closer. There was a chance it was a coincidence, but it was just as likely that someone had heard the Harvesters firing weapons and called the police.

"Tick-tock, Solo," Beatrix said. "Now—"

Whatever she was about to say was cut short. From the shadows around the industrial freezers, Shane saw Cassius' hulking form. Beatrix had her back to the ghost, but Shane had just a few seconds to react as the ghost hurled a large object toward them.

A silver cylinder tumbled through the air, trailing a thick, ever-expanding cloud of white behind it. The escaping gas hissed loudly and propelled the cylinder forward toward Shane and Beatrix.

Shane turned and ran. She hadn't shot him so far, so he felt his odds were better dealing with her than the condensed gas canister that approached like a hand grenade.

Shane knew what was coming. Cassius had broken open another nitrogen tank by destroying the valve. He didn't look back to see if Beatrix realized what was happening. The tank hit the ground with a metallic clink and then burst with earthshaking force.

Liquid nitrogen rolled out across the floor, expanding at an unbelievable pace as it changed states from liquid to gas and increased in size hundreds and hundreds of times over. The wave rolled across the dead woman on the floor, freezing her and the pool of blood around her in the blink of an eye.

The blast of freezing air that hit Shane was paradoxically like fire. He put enough distance between himself and the tank to avoid the liquid as it expanded, but as it turned to gas, the cloud rolled over him as cold as anything he'd ever felt.

He gasped as the white mist climbed up his shoulders and the top of his head. His lungs burned, and he couldn't draw any oxygen. He realized that the nitrogen had pushed out the breathable air with explosive force. All he could do was hold his breath and continue running, putting distance between himself and the glacial fog that overwhelmed him.

"Here," August said, appearing in the murk.

The ghost grabbed Shane by the wrist, the cold of his dead flesh not nearly as freezing as the nitrogen licking at his heels. With a forceful pull, August jerked Shane toward a window that looked out over the parking lot.

Shane smashed through the pane, clearing away the glass, then jumped and tumbled into the parking lot, taking the brunt of the fall on his shoulder. He hit the ground with a grunt and rolled through the shards of broken glass until he was free of them.

White mist billowed through the missing window above him. The sirens got louder, and he knew the police would be there at any moment.

Beatrix, the gunman, and the third man were either dead or had left the building in a different direction. The ghost had cleared everyone with one move, and there was no way to get back to him without getting caught.

Shane got to his feet and started running with August at his side.

"Where are we going?" the ghost asked, looking back at the window they had just escaped from.

"Hear that?" Shane gestured in the direction of the siren. The ghost nodded. They reached the edge of the plant, then turned the corner and ran toward the train tracks at the rear. "We're going away from that."

Shane was only halfway to the fence when the first police car raced into the parking lot with lights flashing. He ducked into the shadows, August hiding with him, as they waited for the second police vehicle to pass them by. The police were heading to the front entrance, but if any more backup came, they would check the rear soon enough.

As soon as the cars had passed them, Shane headed for the fence. He climbed it and made his way to the train tracks beyond. There was no sign of the Harvesters at the back of the building, and he knew the ghost was still inside. There was no reason for Cassius to flee. He had the upper hand, and he had time to plot his next move.

There was only one place to go. Winston's house was the center of everything. Cassius' haunted item would be there somewhere, and there was just as strong a likelihood that the Harvesters had retreated there as well if they had survived the nitrogen.

Once the police investigated the plant and discovered two new dead bodies, Ocean Imperial Fish would be a crime scene, the location of several deaths in just a couple of days. That meant law enforcement would be crawling over the neighborhood soon enough.

He needed to lure Cassius out of the plant without the police or the Harvesters seeing him, and Winston's house was the best place to take the ghost to finish the job. It was the only place Shane was sure he had some degree of control over, and August knew all the ins and outs. It was just a matter of how he could trick the big ghost into going back there.

Shane wished he knew more about the ghost's history. August knew he was violent, and a killer, but that was already evident and not useful. Shane was going into this fight almost blind, and he had the Harvesters and the police to worry about at the same time.

"Where are we going?" August asked.

"Back to Winston's," Shane answered as they finished crossing the tracks and hit the open fields behind the residential neighborhood.

"But what about the Harvesters and Cassius?"

"We're going back to Winston's," Shane repeated. "There's nothing else we can do here with the police. Cassius knows we're after him, so he's going to be impossible to get out of there now. He has the advantage. We have to make him come to us."

"But why would he come to us if he has the advantage in the factory?"

"Because he doesn't want to be there. It's a stopover for him, a safe house for the time being. Once the police are done with the plant, it will be an empty building with nothing to keep his attention. You said this ghost was locked in a box for decades, right? He's going to want to be out in the world and making up for lost time."

"But he was imprisoned by Mr. Winston. Why would he ever come back here?" August countered.

They moved swiftly over the rough terrain, putting as much space between themselves and the police as possible. Shane saw nothing of the Harvesters along the way and suspected they had at least one additional base of operations somewhere in the area.

"Winston's house is familiar," Shane said. "It's home, for lack of a better word. Prison or not, it's going to call to him. It was the center of his universe, and he'll feel safe there. He'll feel confident. And with Winston dead, he's going to feel free. He'll want to make it his own."

Shane didn't think August was sold on that idea, but August's experience as a ghost was different from most Shane had met. He was more of a rent-a-friend than a spirit, and he wasn't haunting Winston's house, just living there.

The house was quiet when they returned. Shane stayed out of sight as best he could, not wanting to draw attention from the neighbors as he circled the perimeter, checking windows and searching the front for signs of the Harvesters.

If Beatrix and the others had survived and fled the factory, they had not come back to the house. As near as Shane could see, the coast was clear.

"Have a look to make sure," he advised August, waiting for the ghost to do a sweep of the interior. August was gone for only a few minutes before he returned to where Shane waited at the rear of the house.

"It looks the same as when we left," the ghost said.

"Good. Then we regroup here. We need the police presence to die down and give the Harvesters a chance to make another mistake. They've lost two already. The woman might not be rattled, but the other two are."

"If Cassius hasn't killed them," August said. He wasn't wrong.

The smell inside the house had not improved. Shane sat at the dining room table with the rear blinds open just enough for him to see the backyard. The position also gave him a view down a hall toward the front room. If anyone came through the door, he'd see them and have time to react before they saw him.

He did little so as not to draw attention, waiting out the hours in the dining room as the world outside kept on spinning. August was antsy but had little to say until midnight approached.

"So, we're just going to wait here and do nothing?" August asked as Shane leaned back on one of the dining room chairs. "We can do something and still avoid the police, can't we? They're nowhere near here."

"Those are two fresh bodies in that factory," Shane said. "The nitrogen was just dissipating when they arrived. They know a killer is nearby, and this is the closest neighborhood. It's not safe to wander around looking suspicious."

"For how long?" August asked as though Shane had an answer.

"Somewhere you need to be?" Shane replied.

"No, it's just…"

The ghost stopped talking, and Shane, at first, took it to mean he had nothing more to say. But he saw the ghost's expression change as he looked at something over Shane's shoulder.

Shane turned and looked toward the front room where Winston's body rotted. Something moved in the shadows, and Shane tensed. He held up a finger to silence August when he saw the ghost about to say something and waited for another sign of movement. Whatever was in the living room was quiet and moving very carefully.

There were brief flashes of something dark, low to the ground, and quick, hidden behind the furniture. Shane watched until it rounded the edge of a table and came into view.

"What is that?" August whispered.

Shane watched the thing in the doorway turn at the sound of the ghost's voice. He was wondering the same thing.

CHAPTER 11
THE HOUNDS

The ghost looked like it had been broken, healed, and then broken again and again. Shane had seen many spirits that had returned as something impossible. But the creature that slinked out of the living room looked like it had been made intentionally. Like someone had tried to turn what was once human into an animal.

It walked on all fours, and fragments of broken ribs pierced its back along its spine on either side like a ridge of spikes on its back. The knees and ankles had been broken and bent in the wrong direction. Its feet were turned backward, and a break had been inflicted in the upper arms that allowed them to bend both ways as it moved, giving it a swaying, gangly gait.

Someone had carefully peeled the flesh from the creature's face. Shane could not tell if it had once been male or female given the amount of trauma. A distinct outline exposed the skull and created the effect of spikes above the eyes and along the cheekbones.

The nose, lips, cheeks, and most of the lower face had been excised. Only polished bone remained, bright white and clean. The eyes remained in bony sockets with no lids or muscle holding them in place. The effect was shocking and made it look like the bloodshot orbs would tumble from the skull at any moment.

The ghost had its bulging eyes fixed on Shane, and they stared at each other for a long moment. It had no lips with which to smile, but it chattered its teeth, a quick repetitive clicking motion that preceded a full run.

"Mother of God," August whispered.

Though its limbs had been broken in multiple places and it was on all fours, the ghost ran like nothing Shane had ever encountered. It covered the space between them in a flash, leaping like a predator on prey as it reached the kitchen with its ragged hands extended like claws.

It threw itself onto Shane with no regard for strategy or self-preservation. It used its entire body as a weapon and slammed into him with enough force to knock him back against the table.

The lipless mouth snapped and bit on Shane's sleeve, narrowly missing flesh. It snapped again, trying for his neck, but he held it at bay.

It fought with its hands and feet, raking him with thick, curled toenails and long, ragged, fingernails. Because of all the broken bones, Shane couldn't move its arms away the way he would have with a living opponent or a normal ghost. Holding it by the wrists or at the shoulders proved ineffective because of its rubbery appendages.

Claws raked along his arms, and when it got closer, they sank into his shoulders and back. He did his best to force the ghost's face away, but it sunk its teeth into his cheek, biting down with enough force to remove a small chunk.

The ghost was like an attack dog, some feral thing that had found a morsel of food and was already taken by the madness of starvation. Shane wrestled with it on the floor, unsure where August had gone or what he was up to. He rolled back and forth with the creature, looking for something vulnerable that he could hold onto so it would stop attacking.

Pain seared his arms and thighs where fingernails and toenails dug into him. He soon abandoned his usual fighting tactics and just tried to overpower the ghost with brutality.

Shane grabbed hold of the ghost's upper arms and rolled it roughly to the ground as he moved with it, getting his body on top. He ignored the scratching claws and went straight for its face, plunging his thumbs into the bulging eyes that stared wildly.

A horrible, wordless howl escaped the ghost's throat. It was like a warbling cry of panic and anger as Shane sunk its eyes into its skull and forced his body weight onto both arms.

He growled as a bent thumbnail, cold as ice, hooked into his collarbone and dug under the flesh and muscle. The lipless mouth of the ghost was parted wide in an endless wail. Shane's fingers grasped the half-flayed skull, and he pushed with all his might.

The skull buckled and gave way with a wet crunch. The ghost's head collapsed under Shane's weight and burst to the sides in a thick spray of blood, brain, and bone. It lasted for only a fraction of a second and then the ghost's body ruptured with a furious blast of energy that shot Shane backward and shook the room.

Shane landed hard and lay on his side on the floor, wind knocked from his lungs. It took a moment to catch his breath as the pain from the explosion radiated through his body as though he'd been hit by a car.

He stayed still for another beat, his face resting on the cold linoleum. His eyes fixed on nothing in particular until his pulse slowed and his breathing evened out. August came to him, crouching low and reaching out a hand.

"Do you need to go to the hospital?" he asked, looking Shane over.

"I'm fine," he answered. "It's nothing."

He sat up slowly, feeling the pain dissipate as he breathed deeply. A noise from the front room drew his attention as a second ghost came running down the hallway. This one, though not identical to the first, must have come from the same place.

Someone had carved into the new spirit's face, much like the first one, but the shape of the wound was different. A strip of flesh three fingers wide had been removed from the ghost's chin up its face and across its bald skull. The skin on either side was swollen and red, but the missing segment had been cleaned down to the bone.

The new spirit ran on all fours as the first one had, and its bones were broken much the same. Its limbs were like rubber as it bounded down the hall toward Shane. There was no way it could have been supporting itself, and yet, it was.

"Jesus," Shane muttered, getting quickly to his feet as the new monstrosity closed the gap between them. It rose to meet Shane, reaching out with broken hands. Shane caught its wrists, but the ghost leaned in, using its momentum to push its head forward as its jaw hung low and a flood of rancid, thick blood spewed from its mouth and across his face and chest.

The smell was stomach-turning, and the blood was hot as it cascaded down his torso. Shane ignored it, holding fast to the ghost's wrists so it couldn't claw at him.

He struggled with the ghost, holding it at arm's length as it jerked and thrashed to free itself. Like the first ghost, it moved not like a human, but an animal. Caught in Shane's grasp, it was like a rabid beast, pulling and writhing with so much force that he could barely hold on.

The ghost spread its jaws as it fought to free itself from Shane's grasp. Its body jerked left and right, and its head seemed to be working in the opposite direction as a second flood of bloody vomit escaped, spraying Shane's face and chest again.

August looked like he was on the verge of vomiting, shouting at the spirit to let Shane go but not physically interfering. Shane pushed the ghost off as it began to let loose a third blast of vomit, avoiding the spray but giving the ghost the chance to lunge at him again.

He raised his arms to block the assault and brought an elbow down hard on the ghost head, forcing it low and allowing it to attack his waist and drag them both to the ground.

The wet, rumbling moan belched forth once more as another stream of viscous, dead sludge splattered across Shane. They rolled in it on the floor, and it prevented Shane from regaining his footing to mount an adequate counterattack. The two squirmed like fish out of water, with the broken monstrosity scrambling for Shane's throat.

Shane lashed out at the ghost, jamming the tips of his fingers under the ridge of flesh that was scabbed along the polished bone strip. The cold skin gave way, and his hand slipped between the ghost's face and skull, causing it to bulge and pull away.

He pushed his hands deep under the ghost's face until the tips of his fingers reached its ear at the back of its jaw. Shane curled his fingers and pulled hard, separating the jawbone and allowing him to grip and pull.

The next blast of vomit came out with a pained howl as Shane pried the ghost's lower jaw off its skull with a snap. The hot, bloody surge gushed out over the ghost's neck and chest without the force of the previous flows.

With the jawbone still in his hand, Shane thrust up through the roof of the spirit's mouth, forcing the broken bone inside its skull. The ghost's awkward cry ended immediately as the skull cracked. Shane's free hand came down on the top of its head, popping it like an overripe tomato.

The force of the explosion caused Shane to glide through the pool of rancid vomit as it vanished along with the ghost's remains. He came to a stop against the refrigerator, breathing heavily but no longer saturated in the foul-smelling liquid.

August was at his side immediately, no longer hesitant to make contact as he grabbed Shane's shirt in his hands and shook him to get his attention.

"You have to get up," he shouted. "There's another one."

He moved aside and pointed toward the living room. The third spirit was not on the ground like the other two had been: This one crawled on the wall like an insect. It was impossibly long and thin, as though it had no muscle mass, just jaundiced flesh over thick-jointed bones.

This ghost had been skinned. It had a perfectly polished, white skull without an ounce of flesh or muscle. Even the eyes were missing, but the empty sockets were pointed in Shane's direction.

"How many of these things are there?" Shane said, getting back to his feet.

Pain throbbed in his chest from the explosions he'd just absorbed. The Harvesters had to be sending the spirits, but he couldn't keep facing them like this. Even if he defeated them, the damage he suffered each time would compound until he couldn't go on.

The insect-like ghost on the wall didn't make a move as Shane got to his feet. They watched each other, the spirit observing Shane while he steadied himself. Once he was upright, the ghost reached its long limbs for the far wall. It braced itself, suspended above the floor, and then scuttled forward.

Shane's instinct was to fight. To meet the creeping monstrosity head-on and destroy it as he had the others. But if he did, and another came, and another, and another, he would die soon enough.

The ghost burst from the hallway, arms and legs splayed wide like a mantis. Shane turned and ran.

CHAPTER 12

HUNTMASTER

Shane slammed through the door and stumbled out onto the back lawn of Winston's house. The night air was cool, and it was a relief to get away from the stench of the house, even if he was only doing so to run for his life. He ran to the side of the house and then back toward the front, intent on getting to his car.

August followed closely behind as they passed into the front yard. Shane was bathed in white light the moment he was in view of Winston's driveway.

Beatrix stood in the driveway with the gunman from the Ocean Imperial Fish plant. The third man was inside a black car behind the SUV that had its lights trained on Shane. August froze and Shane came to a halt with him. The smile on the woman's face was exactly the expression Shane would have expected. Smug, confident, and far too pleased with herself.

"Look what the cat dragged in," Beatrix said.

Next to her, the gunman had his weapon drawn and aimed. He said nothing, but his arm seemed less shaky than it had the first time they met.

The spindly, insect-like ghost rounded the corner behind Shane and August. It was crawling on the exterior wall of the house and leaped toward Shane when it had no wall left on which to attach itself.

Shane braced himself for a fight. At the last minute, the ghost twisted in mid-air as Beatrix blew a whistle, causing it to flop awkwardly to Shane's left and scramble away.

The ghost ran to the woman's side, its long, thin arms and legs bent awkwardly as it huddled next to her like a dog she'd called to heel. The empty eyes remained fixed on Shane, but it held still as a statue next to Beatrix. Shane wondered how many others she still had handy.

"Look what we have here," Beatrix said. She was not referring to Shane this time. Instead, her sly smile was focused on August. "You got away from me, you sneaky little snake."

August looked dumbfounded and said nothing. Beatrix found amusement in that. She took a step forward and August remained where he was, staring back at her like a man on the edge of a cliff deciding when to jump.

"You are part of the whole," she said. "I'm not done here if I don't have you in the bag."

"The hell does that even mean?" Shane asked, getting her to focus on him again.

"What do you think it means, genius?" she shot back.

He glanced at the gunman. He still had Shane in his sights, and the deformed ghost was just as focused.

"You think there's sport in that? He's a chef," Shane said.

"A dead one."

"It doesn't make him special."

"He's part of the group. I need him to finish the hunt."

Shane scoffed.

"You're like those jackasses that shoot deer out of season. As long as you get to throw down, huh? Thought only guys who can't get laid and have overpriced sports cars acted like that."

Beatrix chuckled and took another step toward them. She was still focused on August but spared Shane a glance.

"You'll get your chance soon enough, Solo, don't worry. I just wanted to get closer to our little friend here."

She lifted her hand, and August flinched. The nervous movement made her laugh, and once he realized she hadn't touched him, that's when she made her move, lightly giving him a tap on the cheek.

"He's right about you, isn't he? You're just a little coward. Never killed anyone before, have you?" she said.

"Of course not," August sputtered. "Why would I have?"

"Dog-eat-dog world and all that," she replied with a shrug.

They were almost nose to nose, and August looked like he might turn and run at any moment. Beatrix reached out and adjusted his hair, pushing a tiny, stray lock behind his ear.

"I just want to live," he said to her. She laughed loudly at that, a genuine sound full of mirth.

"What the hell does that mean? You're already dead," she pointed out.

"I just... it's not right. I never hurt anyone. Mr. Winston never hurt anyone. Why did you have to do this?"

It was the boldest Shane had ever seen the ghost. Not bold enough to raise a hand against her, and he still looked like he would wet himself if he could do such a thing anymore, but at least he was speaking up. There was some aggression in his voice, some passion there. Beatrix was finally making him angry.

"I didn't," she said.

The brief answer caught August by surprise. He probably hadn't expected a real answer, and definitely not that one.

"What do you mean?" he asked.

"I didn't have to do... this." She gestured around them.

"Then why did you?"

August was incredulous, and his anger was rising. Beatrix was baiting him, and he didn't realize it. Shane, still at gunpoint, was not willing to jump into anything just yet. In all honesty, he was curious about her answer.

"Because he paid me to," she said, hiking her thumb backward.

It was not clear if she was referring to the gunman or the man in the vehicle. Shane assumed it was the coward still hidden in the car behind the SUV. The gunman seemed more like a business associate than a client. But the coward? If this was a hunt, Shane could see him being the sort of guy who paid someone to hunt a ghost for him.

"What grudge did Mr. Spineless have against Winston?" Shane asked.

Beatrix glanced at Shane and then looked over her shoulder at the car for a minute, chuckling.

"He's a bit of a wuss, isn't he?" she said, more to herself than the others. "Not my pig, not my farm, though. He paid, he gets the services requested."

"Sounds very honorable," Shane told her.

"Oh no," she said, her voice suddenly mocking. "My honor has been questioned by a hairless freak and his nancy ghost. What will I do?"

She rolled her eyes and refocused on August.

"You're my bonus, Slim Jim. Wussy only wanted the big fella; the rest of you are the cost of doing business. And after losing Kraft and Tully, my costs are very high. I'm going to enjoy putting an end to you."

She reached out and took hold of August by the throat, her fingers around the back of his neck with her thumb pressed against his windpipe as she stared into his eyes.

"Please don't," he whispered.

"Please don't what?" she hissed.

August closed his eyes. His hands were trembling, he looked like a mortal man facing his demise. Shane had never come across a ghost so terrified.

"Please don't kill me," he begged.

"Please don't kill me," Beatrix repeated in a whiny, mocking tone. "I told you, you're already dead."

"I don't care," the ghost replied.

Beatrix pressed the tip of her thumb harder against August's throat and stared at him without saying anything for a long moment. Shane kept his focus on her while watching the gunman in his peripheral vision. He was still alert and aiming at Shane.

"Did you know that Big Boy is turning out to be a real wild card? He's already killed a dozen people. Cops in town are having a panic attack over this one, and I don't like dealing with cops. I wouldn't have to deal with them if you hadn't got in my way," she said.

August said nothing, keenly aware of the hand on his throat and the danger he was in.

"What would you do if I let you go?" she asked suddenly.

August was confused by the question and didn't have an immediate answer. She pressed her thumb harder into his windpipe.

"What would you do?"

"I'd run!" he blurted. "I'd leave."

"Where to?" she asked.

"What?"

"Where will you run where I can't find you?" she wanted to know.

August had not prepared an answer for that and could only shake his head weakly. Shane did not like the feeling that had formed in his gut.

"I don't know," the ghost answered.

Beatrix smiled, and it was cold and unsettling.

"You better think fast, then."

She let him go and took a step back. She looked from August to Shane and back and nodded as though she was hearing something the rest of them could not.

"I don't understand," August said.

Shane understood. He could see the resolve on her face and the plan unfolding in her head.

"She wants us to run," Shane told him.

"Yes," she confirmed, grinning widely. "That's exactly what I want."

"To run? Run where? Why?" August asked.

"I lost two men today," Beatrix said. "I'm owed two bodies. You two will have to do, won't you?"

"We didn't kill them," August protested. "That had nothing to do with us."

"Five minutes. You fast, Solo?" Beatrix asked.

"Does it matter?"

"It'll matter to you. I'm being fair here. I'm giving you a sporting chance. Down to four minutes and forty-five seconds. I'd get moving if I were you."

Shane said nothing. He turned and ran, leaving August behind as he headed up the driveway to the street.

August was slow on the uptake but followed soon after Shane fled the property. The ghost caught up one house down while Shane made a beeline for his car. He wasn't sure where he could get in four minutes, but it was better than nothing.

"What the hell is going on?" August demanded. "Is she going to hunt both of us now?"

"That's exactly what's going on," Shane said.

He cursed before reaching the car. Under the streetlight, he saw the flaccid outline of the rear tires. Somehow, they had known it was his car and slashed them all. They would not be driving to safety.

"What's nearby?" Shane asked.

"What?"

He turned to the ghost and took him by the shoulders in the middle of the dark street.

"Wake the hell up, August. Your friend died, your world fell apart, you're not a fighter or an adventurer or anything. I don't care. You need to get your head out of your ass, or we are both going to die out here, do you understand me?"

August blinked, and Shane shook him harshly.

"That way," the ghost stammered, pointing to a road at Shane's back that led away from Winston's street.

"What's that way?"

"Houses. Places to hide. A golf course," August answered.

Shane clapped the ghost on the shoulder.

"Golf course? Good. Lead the way."

The two of them ran, Shane pumping his legs as fast as he could and wishing not for the first time that he would have considered smoking less. He pushed himself even as he felt his chest burning, taking a right, then a left, then a right again to make it harder for Beatrix and the gunman to follow.

Winston lived in a quiet, affluent neighborhood. The streets were mostly empty save for the odd dog walker that Shane ran past. Many houses and yards could have been potential hiding places, but Shane did not want to put civilians in jeopardy. He knew Beatrix would not think twice about killing someone if they got between her and her targets.

"The golf course is this way." August pointed, taking them down a tree-lined road with wide sidewalks and exceptional landscaping.

The five minutes were certainly up, but Shane had not seen or heard any sign of Beatrix and the others. He did not expect that she was a woman to make idle threats. She would come after them, and her goal was to kill Shane and destroy August.

"There's no place to hide on the golf course," August said. "It's empty space."

"That's good," Shane told him. "No place for them to hide, either. No way for someone else to get hurt."

He did not have a very well-thought-out plan. He just expected the golf course to be empty at night so there would be no collateral damage from other people. Beyond that, he hadn't considered what he would do. It was just one last thing to worry about. He could only rely on August's knowledge of the neighborhood to help them come out on top.

Shane's feet pounded the pavement, and his breath was heavy and strained in his ears, merging with the sound of rustling leaves and night birds in the treetops. As the breeze died down, Shane realized he was producing the only sounds on the street. The birds had fallen silent, and

August made no sound.

Shane glanced over his shoulder as he ran. The streetlights flickered behind him, and then went out, one by one. As each one buzzed and went dead, he caught the barest glimpse of something at the edges of the light. Something low to the ground and long-limbed.

They had been found.

CHAPTER 13

RUN FOR YOUR LIFE

The insect-like ghost rushed Shane. Streetlights buzzed and died along the way as it approached until the entire street was plunged into darkness. Shane watched as the gangly creature jumped at him, extending its arms and legs like it was taking flight.

Shane tried to catch it and use its momentum to throw the ghost off-balance, but its long arms still latched onto him. Its legs did the same, wrapping around him like secondary arms and he was caught in the ghost's embrace as he shook it off.

The ghost squeezed, using its arms and hands for leverage and pulling on them as though it were pulling a knot tight. The bare skull inched closer while Shane kept his hands firmly planted against the ghost's collarbone, his fingers hooked over its shoulders to keep it at bay.

Shane's legs got tangled in the ghost's, and he stumbled. The ghost snaked one leg between Shane's and tripped him, causing them to fall to the pavement with the ghost on top.

The lipless mouth clacked and snapped as it tried to bite. It opened its mouth wider as its arms and legs drew Shane in.

Frustrated by the confinement of the arms holding him tightly, Shane shifted his weight and forced them to roll until he was on top of the ghost. With his arms still extended, he waited until it spread its jaws wide in anticipation of lunging and gnashing.

The moment the ghost lowered its skeletal jaw, Shane lifted his left arm and forced his elbow between its teeth. With its mouth already fully extended, it lost its control to do damage as he crammed his elbow to the back of its throat.

The ghost struggled and thrashed beneath him. It pulled its arms free, trying to grab hold of Shane's arm and dislodge it. Free from its strangling grasp, Shane swung his other arm like a hammer, slamming the butt of his hand on his other arm that protruded from the clean, white jaws.

The joint snapped first and then the skull as Shane's elbow broke through the roof of the ghost's mouth and crushed its head from the inside out. The explosion of energy was swift and brutal, launching Shane onto August, who was caught by surprise and tumbled back to the ground with him.

August was first to his feet, and he pulled Shane up with him.

"She's got to be close. We need to go," he urged, yanking on Shane's wrist.

Shane nodded as he took a moment to catch his breath and then got to his feet. Three ghosts in a row with very little time between was not easy to deal with. His body had no choice but to absorb the damage when they exploded. He had never been certain what sort of energy was released, but it kicked like a horse. He didn't know if he could handle a fourth without more time to recuperate.

August urged him on, pointing out how close they were to the golf course every few paces. The street behind them remained dark. If Beatrix was following, she did so silently and with the same limited vision Shane had. Except, as he recalled, she had thermal imaging technology.

At the end of the street, they reached a driveway that led into the golf course and wound up to the north toward what Shane assumed was a parking lot and the clubhouse. He ignored it and took the southern route across the greens and onto the open, empty course.

The course was well-maintained and once he left some trees to the side of the green, he found himself in a wide-open fairway that led to the first hole several hundred yards away.

There were no lights on the course and no way for anyone who didn't have thermal cameras to see him. Not all of the Harvesters in the factory had thermal cameras, though. The dead man had one, and the coward had one, so Shane was hoping they had a limited number. He was hoping for anything that might give him a leg up in the situation.

He ran across the fairway with August in tow and then hit the rough, trudging across the longer grass toward the cover of more trees.

"How big is this course?" Shane asked as he darted around a copse of elms.

"Eighteen holes," August said.

Shane scoffed and shook his head, looking back the way they had come. He saw nothing moving.

"How wide. How far to the other side?" he clarified.

"Oh. I have no idea. I've never been to the other side," August said.

"Too far to travel?" Shane asked.

The ghost nodded. It was beyond the mile radius he could normally travel from Winston's house. He'd have no further insight on what to do or where to go.

Not that he had been especially helpful so far.

Shane found himself caught between frustration and something close to sympathy for the ghost. He was so out of his depth out in the world. When he had been alive, August was a timid man who didn't like to ruffle feathers. In death, Winston had shielded him from the world. He never became a ghost the way others did. He was more of a servant on demand or a friend for an old man who didn't get along well with the living.

There was something undeniably pathetic about August, but Shane couldn't just abandon him. It was rare to come across a ghost that was so civil, so much like he must have been in life. Someone who just wanted to be left alone to do the simple things he did. Carl and Eloise had more edge to them than August. Even Herbert did.

Shane paused at a large golden maple and doubled over to catch his breath. August stopped with him and the two remained quiet for a long moment.

"Thank you for doing this," the ghost said.

Shane looked him in the eye. The ghost must have read something on his face, gleaned something from his body language. That was something if it was true. Maybe he had some instincts after all.

"I said I'd help," Shane said.

"You did. But you didn't know it would turn out like this. I never would have asked for help if I thought things would go this way."

Shane shrugged.

"Your friend was murdered. I didn't think I was coming here just to express my dissatisfaction."

"I suppose so," August agreed. "I just wish it was different. This is too much. Why are they doing this?"

"Money," Shane said. "The weak guy—the one who bolted first at the fish factory—this is his game. He lost control, though. Got out of hand, and now he's spooked. But this Beatrix is hardcore. He's scared of her, and she doesn't think she needs to give up yet."

"How do you know that?"

"She said she got paid. He clearly doesn't want to be here anymore, but he has to be. She might have threatened him; I don't know. My guess is he thought he was a tough guy, heard about this ghost hunt, and figured it'd be some real bad-ass adventure. A something-no-one-else-has-done sort of thing. Until Cassius proved too much."

"But why Mr. Winston? He was a good man," August lamented. Shane could only shrug.

"If you don't recognize the guy, then I don't know. Maybe he had dealings with Winston when you weren't there. Or someone who knows about Cassius told this guy. People in this world talk more than you'd think. Especially the dead. Someone knew Winston had that ghost locked up, and they knew why. It got back to our cowardly hunter, and he probably dropped a lot of cash to make this happen before it blew up in his face."

"But no one knew," August assured him.

"Someone always knows," Shane said. It was true no matter how much August didn't want to believe it. The fact Beatrix and her Harvesters had come for him proved it.

Shane stood and nodded into the distance across another fairway.

"Let's keep going," he said. The more distance they had between them and the others, the better. If they could shake her, they might even get a chance to get back to the ghost in the fish factory. Maybe.

They made their way to another tree-lined rough across the next fairway when a high-pitched howl cut through the silence. Shane thought for a moment that Beatrix had sent another ghost after them but soon realized it was not a crazed, feral spirit. It was Beatrix.

"Gonna have to run faster than that!"

Her words rang out through the darkness, seeming to come from more than one direction. Shane ignored her and pushed harder, darting past trees and shrubs to another open patch of neatly trimmed grass.

"She's going to catch us," August said nervously.

Shane's eyes darted right as he ran, focusing on something in the distance.

"There," he said, pointing. Long, green reeds and cattails lined the edges of a small pond, the first water hazard he'd seen on the course.

"What?" the ghost asked as he switched directions and raced toward the pond.

"Just move," Shane said.

Beatrix let loose a long, celebratory howl in the distance that broke into laughter. Shane reached the edge of the pond but didn't stop, running headlong into the water and taking a sharp right around the reeds and cattails as he submerged himself quickly and quietly, venturing farther and farther from the shore.

"What the hell are you doing?" August demanded. Shane waved him forward, and August reluctantly joined him, slipping below the surface without a ripple.

"She's coming!" the ghost hissed, keeping his voice down. Shane nodded, immersing himself in the reeds until only his head was out of the water.

"Stay under the water until I say it's clear," Shane said. "If this doesn't work, you're better off hiding in the mud."

The seconds ticked by, and Beatrix continued her taunts as she grew closer. She hooted and laughed and shouted the odd insult. Shane scooped mud from the bottom of the pond. It felt like putty in his hands, and he smeared it across the top of his head and face and then lowered until his nose was barely above the surface.

Beatrix's voice grew louder. From the reeds, Shane caught a glimpse of movement. After a deep breath, he lowered into the pond, his face inches below the surface. He could see only darkness and the distorted shapes of reeds around him. He hoped August was still submerged and keeping still.

Every moment felt too long and drawn out. He feared he'd ducked under too soon, that his lungs would give out, and he'd be forced to emerge and be caught. He focused on the time, on keeping calm, and the rate of his heartbeat.

A shimmering light appeared in the distance, wavering strangely through the prism of the water above his face. It was attached to a shape. He held still and watched the distorted image of the gunman walk to the edge of the pond, holding one of the tablets. Beatrix came with him, and he heard her shout again, the sound muffled by the water. They continued along the shoreline, away from Shane and deeper into the golf course.

His lungs felt compressed by fire. Too much running and too many cigarettes were taking their toll, but he had to stay hidden. He could not see them, but they were close.

He forced a calm on himself. He ignored the pressure and screaming in his lungs demanding he rise those few inches and take a breath, letting another second pass.

Five seconds. Fifteen.

As quietly as he could, Shane let his head emerge, careful to not splash or make a sound. Any potential ripples could be blamed on the stems of the reeds, and perhaps a turtle or a frog moving from the shore.

He drew in a long breath, trying to keep it silent and calm. He could hear Beatrix on the far side of the pond. She was shouting out to him, but the sound grew more distant. He stayed frozen in the water until she had put enough distance between herself and the pond that Shane felt she would no longer hear his movements.

August popped up after him, moving soundlessly at his side.

"They didn't see us. That was a good idea," the ghost remarked.

Shane nodded. He didn't bother to tell August that he wasn't sure it would work, and he was just as likely to have been spotted and shot. He was glad it went to plan.

"Let's get moving," Shane said.

They still had a killer ghost to catch.

CHAPTER 14
BACKTRACK

"How long before they come back?" August asked.

They were running back the way they had come, tracing their footsteps back to Winston's house.

"I have no idea," Shane answered.

Beatrix had proven unpredictable so far. She did things her way, and that meant it would be hard to guess her next move.

If she was dedicated to the hunt, she was not likely to give up. She'd keep tracking Shane and August for a while, but at some point, she'd realize the trail had gone cold. From there, it was a crapshoot. Maybe she'd do what Shane did and backtrack. Or maybe she had another plan up her sleeve.

Cassius had not stopped killing people. Beatrix wanted to destroy him. He was becoming a real prize for someone like her. But she needed to catch him, too. She couldn't let him go on a rampage indefinitely if she expected to do her job and get away unseen.

Shane didn't like dealing with so many unknowns. He knew too little about Cassius to form a real plan of attack. And he didn't like splitting his time between focusing on the ghost and Beatrix.

She had to have had a plan when she let Shane and August go. At least he thought she did. But maybe she was just crazy enough to gamble on catching them on skill alone with no backup plan in place. Hell, maybe she had already accepted their escape as a possibility and didn't care.

They emerged onto Winston's street and there was still no sign of Beatrix or her gunman partner. Shane glanced at his car, its flat tires rendering it useless, and had another thought. They knew it was Shane's car. Maybe Beatrix knew more about him than she'd let on. Maybe letting him go wasn't as big a risk as it seemed. Not if she had an idea who Shane was and where he might go.

She held more cards in this game than Shane did: the coward who hired her, the secret of Cassius, and Shane's identity. She seemed reckless, maybe even unstable, but Shane suspected some of that was just for show. There was more going on with Beatrix than she wanted people to see. That meant Shane needed to be even more cautious than usual.

The neighborhood was still quiet and dark. The Harvesters had left their vehicles in Winston's driveway, so Shane was not certain what had happened to the cowardly man who had apparently hired them. He was no longer in the car, and he hadn't gone with Beatrix. Shane wrote the license plate numbers of the two vehicles on a scrap of paper from his wallet that was still mostly dry after his excursion into the pond. It might come in handy in figuring out who the man who hired Beatrix was.

"What are we doing back here? They caught us once, they'll do it again," August said.

"We can't just bail. Cassius is still killing, and he's not going to stop. Beatrix knows where his haunted item is but doesn't seem willing to shut him down, so we need to focus on him. She'll come back looking for him soon enough. Our best chance is at night if he's still in those factories. Fewer people means fewer victims."

"And the police?" August asked.

"A problem, but not the end of the world. But if Cassius gets it in his head to start killing cops, this could get out of hand fast. When a ghost is willing to kill anyone and everyone, it turns into chaos real quick. Most of the living don't know how to deal with a problem like that."

"How do they deal with it?" August asked.

"More people. Cops, soldiers, people with itchy trigger fingers. It'll mean more deaths."

"Why would they send more people after a murderous ghost? Why not just abandon the area?"

Shane snorted, sneaking around behind Winston's property once more.

"You really have led an isolated death, haven't you?"

"Insulting me doesn't answer the question," the ghost replied evenly.

"It's not an insult; it's an observation. You know that most people don't believe in ghosts, right? That most people can't see them? And most people don't want to believe in them even when they're shown signs. You can't tell the police that the killer they're after is a ghost. They'll think you're crazy."

"But what if they see for themselves? If Cassius keeps going, they'll have to see."

Shane shook his head, leaving the backyard for the field.

"That's not how it works. If one cop saw Cassius and told the others about it, they would think he was crazy. If ten cops saw Cassius and told their superiors, they would think they were crazy. There's no way this works out with everyone believing that there's a supernatural cause," Shane explained.

"But at some point—" August began before Shane cut him off with a wave of his hand.

"The whole police department could get behind the story and then the city, the county, or the state would say it was a cover-up and cops are the ones who committed the crime. Or maybe they're all on drugs together. It doesn't matter. The truth will never be the accepted answer. Meanwhile, the whole time you're trying to prove that a ghost is the killer, he keeps killing. So, what's the better option? That you make the world believe in something they don't want to believe in, or you stop a ghost before he kills one hundred people?"

August seemed unhappy with Shane's explanation and was silent for a long moment as they dashed through the overgrown field toward the railroad tracks.

"It's not fair that he gets to get away with it and no one knows the truth."

"Did you believe in ghosts before you died?" Shane asked.

"Maybe. I never thought about it," he replied.

"Do you know how many people ghosts had killed before you became one?"

"No," August said. "But I never heard anyone even talk about it before. If someone had told me—"

"If someone had told you that, since the beginning of time, vengeful spirits sometimes return and kill anyone unlucky enough to cross their paths, would you have believed it? Would you have signed a petition against it? Formed a posse to root them out even though you can't see them or harm them in any way?"

"Someone could have done something," the dead man protested. "Someone like you, who has the power to take them on."

"Someone like me *does* do something," Shane said. They reached the fence behind Ocean Imperial Fish. "I'm doing it right now."

August did not reply, and Shane focused on the factory. No sound came from the plant, not that he expected it would. From the rear, he could see no police vehicles or lights.

So soon after what happened, and given that other deaths had occurred in the neighborhood the day before, he suspected they were still around. There would be at least one or two officers on the scene keeping an eye on things.

"Can you head in for a quick look?" Shane said.

August gave a reluctant nod. He feared Cassius as much as he feared Beatrix, but he was willing to at least scout the area to look for the ghost.

Shane hid among the weeds behind the fence as he waited for August to do his work. The police would have done a thorough walkthrough of the plant and investigated everything they could have to search for evidence. Cassius might have waited all of that out, but he didn't strike Shane as the type.

Beatrix had said that the ghost had killed at least a dozen people already. To pull that off, he would have either had to kill some of the police when they showed up after Shane had fled, or he had moved to a new location.

If it had happened at Ocean Imperial Fish, Shane felt like there would still be police presence on scene. But something told him that August would come up empty-handed, and they were going to have to search elsewhere.

If he knew where the ghost's haunted object was, it would make things so much easier. Even if he couldn't access it to seal it away, it would make tracking easier. A specific area from where Shane could focus his search.

Beatrix had to have left it somewhere near Winston's house or else she wouldn't keep going back there. He suspected the only reason she moved it was so that she would have control over where it was. No one else would know where to go to shut Cassius down. Effectively, all the murders he was committing were on her. She could have ended it anytime she wanted to, but she hadn't. She let the lion out of the cage because she wanted it to create mayhem. That was the fun of the hunt for her.

Shane heard a siren in the distance, but it did not come closer. Cassius and the Harvesters were being discreet for the time being. He waited patiently for August's return, which took longer than he would have thought. When the ghost finally appeared, it was as Shane expected.

"I didn't see him," the ghost said. "The bodies are gone, but there's still a lot of blood. And two police officers are out front in a car."

"He's moved on. He's not going to stop killing, but he wants to avoid Beatrix. And me too, probably. He knows we can harm him, so he's going to either keep moving or be smarter going forward."

"So, where does that leave us?" August asked.

The ghost looked around nervously at every sound he heard; whether it was leaves rustling in the breeze or an animal scuttling in the underbrush.

"Free, for the moment," Shane answered.

He might not have had an idea where Cassius was, but at least no one was on to them. They weren't being chased, and weren't in immediate danger, so they had room to breathe.

Shane needed to get in Cassius' head. He had been locked up for decades, more than half a century. The world today was a place he didn't know much about. Ghosts were not easily adaptable. They liked routine, and they were creatures of habit. Cassius would want to return to whatever he knew. Whatever felt familiar

From their limited experience, the thing the ghost liked most was violence. He didn't have to attack anyone in the plant when he was there. The reason they had checked out the frozen food factories in the first place was because they were good hiding places. He knew enough to go there to avoid being tracked by the Harvesters, but he still took the risk of exposing himself. The only reason for that was so he could hurt them, because he had the chance to do so. He was more interested in hurting people than saving himself.

Cassius was smart. There was no such thing as thermal cameras when he was last free in the world. He learned quickly what they were and how they were used. If anything, he lured the Harvesters to the fish factory so he could kill them in a place where they couldn't see him. He was hunting advantages even as the Harvesters were hunting him.

Now, he knew Beatrix and Shane could potentially harm him. The factory was compromised by having too much attention on it. He could have stayed and killed the two remaining police officers. But he didn't. Why not?

"What are you thinking?" August asked, interrupting Shane's train of thought.

"Why would Cassius not stay here and kill the cops?" Shane said, voicing the question that had given him pause.

"Fear of being caught?"

"No," Shane said. "He doesn't have that. Why would he care?"

"Fear of… I don't know."

"He's not afraid. He wasn't avoiding anything. He wanted something," Shane said.

"What could he want?"

"Beatrix," Shane said, venturing a guess. "She attacked him first. She's his first real contact with anything since forever. He lured her there to kill her, but she fought back, and it surprised him."

"You both did," August said.

"But I was second string. I wasn't there at the start. She released him. Then she attacked him. He knows she's hunting him, that's why he took her here. He knows what she wants, but he wants to turn it around on her. He's playing a game with her. He's hunting her as much as she's hunting him."

"I don't know what any of that means," August said. "Wouldn't he just go to one of these other factories to hide in the cold? He can't want to be destroyed after being locked up all this time."

"No," Shane agreed. "He doesn't want to be destroyed. But he also doesn't think he can be. You saw how he treated her. He overpowered her. Maybe she could have gotten away if I hadn't interrupted. She might have had a trick or two handy. But to him? She was a victim, and he lost her. He wants her back; he doesn't want to hide."

"So… he's going after her?"

"Yeah. And he knows where to go to do it."

CHAPTER 15

GROUND ZERO

There was only one place that both Cassius and Beatrix were familiar with. One place where each could guarantee they could find the other if they waited long enough. It wasn't Ocean Imperial Fish, and it wasn't Winston's house. It was Cassius' haunted item.

Shane stayed low to the ground as he made his way back toward the railroad tracks. There was little to be seen from the tracks in the dark of night. The field was not lit, and the sky was too cloudy for light from the moon to make its way through. He could only see the scant few houses in the distance that had lights on to illuminate the yards. Cassius was out there somewhere.

He would have more opportunities to harm people in the neighborhood around Winston's house. Whether he would take advantage, Shane couldn't say.

Most people would be asleep at this hour, easy pickings if the ghost just wanted to rack up a body count. If he was looking for more chaos, fear, and panic, he would want the people awake. That would be more likely to draw in Beatrix as well. Screaming people tended to make a scene.

"Do you have any idea where the Harvesters put Cassius' haunted item? Even a guess," Shane asked August.

"I ran before they moved it. I'm sorry, I don't know," he replied.

"Take a guess. Some place close to the house where it could be hidden. Beatrix didn't take it far; she wanted Cassius to have a home turf advantage."

"But it makes no sense," August countered.

"It makes perfect sense if you think you can hunt him down and destroy him. They're both playing a game now, and we're outsiders. We're random complications no one expected, so the meat of this has nothing to do with us. She wants a challenge, and now he does, too."

"I can't understand why anyone would risk their life doing something so insane," the ghost said.

Shane did not want to spend the time explaining human nature to his naïve partner. He just needed a guess.

"You were there for years, August. You know the property and the neighborhood. Think of a place she could have dropped that box to let the ghost loose but still keep it in her control if and when she needed it."

"I don't know," he replied.

"There has to be something," Shane pushed.

"I don't know!" August said forcefully. "I wouldn't even leave it anywhere; I'd just keep it with me."

Shane considered the ghost's words and looked toward Winston's house, lost in the shadows of the night. There was no way it was that easy, was there? It was so obvious that he'd overlooked the idea.

"Maybe that's what she did," he said.

August looked surprised at Shane's shift in tone.

"You think she's carrying it with her?" he asked.

"No, that'd be a risk He'd be on her no matter where she went. But she doesn't need it in her pocket to still have control of it."

Shane jogged down the tracks with August at his side until they were back within range of Winston's house, and then cut away for another journey across the overgrown field in the backyard. The neighborhood was still relatively quiet, and Shane could see no signs of either the Harvesters or Cassius.

Beatrix had to have abandoned the hunt for Shane and August by now. As determined as she was, with the trail so cold, they must have abandoned the golf course. Heading back to the house put him at risk of running into her again, but he wasn't planning to just let her go. If she was there, he'd do what he could to deal with her.

Shane crept along the far side of the house toward the front driveway. He sent August ahead, staying out of sight in case Cassius or Beatrix were there, and had him take a look around.

"There's nothing," the ghost said upon his return. "Looks like no one has been back yet."

Shane peered around the corner at the two vehicles still parked in the driveway. He ventured out, reaching the first and looking in through the window on the passenger side.

"You've got to be kidding me," he muttered.

A lead-lined wooden box sat on its side in the passenger seat, lid open with a tarnished old straight razor with a bone handle half inside of it. It looked for all the world like someone had thrown it onto the seat and forgotten about it. They hadn't even bothered to sit it upright.

"That's it," August said excitedly, coming to Shane's side. "That's the box from the safe."

It was a testament to just how unconcerned Beatrix was about letting Cassius loose and hunting him down again. She had thrown the haunted item into her car and left it there while she went to track him down. Shane could imagine that she had given Cassius the same five-minute head start she had given Shane and August before she went after him.

She understood that Cassius had murdered innocent people. Had murdered her people. By her admission, he had killed at least a dozen now. She had the power to stop him at any time. All she had to do was go back to the car and close the box. But she hadn't done that. She didn't even care that the car could explode if she destroyed Cassius with his item inside it.

Shane took one last scan of the neighborhood. It seemed that the neighbors were all still fast asleep, and he hadn't seen a car pass Winston's house since he first showed up. He tried the car door handle, but it wouldn't open.

"Plan B," he muttered, reaching for a smooth, round rock from the garden. He wrapped it in the damp fabric of his hoodie and then slammed it into the window.

The car alarm screeched to life, and Shane winced. They showed up at the man's house, murdered him, and took the time to set the alarm on their car. Unbelievable.

"What did you do?" August moaned. Shane ignored him and reached through the broken window for the box. He'd still have time to escape if they didn't worry about the small details like getting caught.

Shane barely had time to set his fingers on the box and feel the coolness of the lead and the texture of the wood before an arm wrapped around his neck. The flesh was cold like meat from a refrigerator, and it squeezed tightly as it pulled him away from the vehicle.

The lead box wobbled from his fingertips, remaining in the passenger seat as Cassius dragged Shane from the car and back toward Winston's house.

"Caught a rabbit in my trap, eh?" the big ghost whispered in Shane's ear. He was holding him tightly against his chest, his fleshy arm pinning Shane's throat powerfully and cutting off his oxygen supply.

Cassius lifted Shane from the ground and took him toward the house. He carried him across the driveway and Shane kicked backward, slamming his feet into the ghost's shins to slow him.

The ghost braced the arm choking Shane with his free arm, increasing the pressure and allowing him to press his cold, dead face against Shane's cheek as though they were almost dancing.

"You're a fighter. I love a good fight. Been so long. Been *too* long," he said appreciatively. Shane kicked back again, slamming his heel into Cassius' shin as hard as he could. The ghost didn't even stumble and continued his lumbering, awkward walk toward the door to Winston's house.

The icy arm around Shane's throat was tight enough that he could barely draw a breath. The force made his vision blur. Spots of light danced before his eyes, and the pressure in his skull felt like it might get close to bursting.

"You know what breaks my heart now?" the ghost continued, easing Shane toward the door. "I can't taste anything anymore. I used to be able to taste blood. That salty, coppery taste. But now it's gone. Not even warm on my tongue. They took that from me."

Shane grunted, unable to reply even if he wanted to. The ghost's cheek was right against his, frozen and fleshy, and he spoke his words in a rushed whisper.

"I used to like the warmth. It's so hot inside the guts at first. When they're still alive and you plunge your hands inside. You think it shouldn't feel warm. But it feels like hot soup in there. It feels so good."

Cassius continued to the door and stopped. With Shane in tow, he was not capable of passing through doors and walls like he was used to. He would have to open the door for Shane to pass through.

"Nothing feels warm anymore. I hate it," Cassius said. "I hate what they did to me."

Shane slammed his heels against the ghost's legs again and tried to pry the thick arms away but could find no purchase. He reached for Cassius' hands, for a finger he could maybe break, but the ghost squeezed harder, cutting off his air supply further. Shane relented, and the ghost relaxed, but only just. He didn't want him dead yet, it seemed.

"I gotta put you down to bring you inside," Cassius said, close to a whisper. "I could kill you here. I could pop your head off your neck—it's not as hard as I thought it would be. But I want to take you inside."

Shane grunted and drew calm, level breaths. He could feel his head swimming already, and he knew he was on the brink. If he couldn't keep the air flowing, he'd pass out. He had to relax and play along.

"I never did that before. I should have. I should have taken someone's head off. It bleeds so much. It's fast, oh, it's so fast. I wanted to taste that, but I never got a chance when I could. It's not as good now, but it's still good, you know?"

Shane grunted again and Cassius hummed softly.

"I'm going to peel off your skin. I want you to know that. I'm going to peel off every bit of it. It's hard around the fingers and the toes. And the eyes, too. If you want to keep it neat and tidy, it's very hard."

Shane didn't respond, and Cassius jerked his body as though checking to make sure he was still awake.

"I'm going to let you go now so I can open the door. If you run, I'm going to break your teeth out one by one. Do you understand?"

Shane grunted again, and he could feel the ghost's face move. He was smiling.

"If you're good, it'll only hurt a little, I promise. I can make it hurt so much. You have no idea how much I can make it hurt. I've never met anyone like you. I want to make it last a long time."

He relaxed and lowered Shane to the ground, slowly and carefully easing his arm from around Shane's throat.

When Shane was free, Cassius looked down at him.

"Don't make me hurt you," he said, reaching for the doorknob.

Shane said nothing, looking the big ghost over from head to toe. They were close together in a small space in front of the door to Winston's house. The angle of the spirit and the time he had to act gave him limited options. He needed to make his move as soon as Cassius' attention shifted to the door.

He went low, dropping down and using his shoulder to slam his entire weight into Cassius' left knee, hitting it at a slightly odd angle so it wasn't dead on but close enough.

The ghost was already putting his weight forward to open the door. Shane extended Cassius' knee, snapping the ghostly connective tissue and popping the joint backward. It separated with a crunch.

Cassius seemed like he was going to fall forward but caught himself on the door to stay upright as he growled angrily and reached down with his free hand.

He tried to lift Shane from the ground, but doing so with a broken leg was not ideal. He managed to only grab Shane's hoodie and help him to his feet as the night went quiet and the car alarm finally turned off. Shane punched the ghost in the face, stunning him briefly and breaking free of his grasp.

Shane had the upper hand now, whether Cassius knew it or not. He pulled back for a right cross and stopped as the sound of a gun cocking behind him drew his attention back to the driveway.

"What the hell do you think you're doing, Solo?" Beatrix asked, approaching Shane and Cassius with the gunman at her side. "This one's my kill, and you know it."

Chapter 16
Standoff

Shane took a step back, out of range of Cassius, who was still leaning on the door to keep himself upright. His leg was broken, but he didn't seem put off by the injury.

Shane kept his hands where the gunman could see them and backed off Winston's porch into a garden at the front of the house so he could keep Cassius and Beatrix in sight.

Each of them kept the other two in view, but no one seemed willing to make the first move. Shane knew everyone was thinking the same thing he was: If any of them attacked, the other two could gain the upper hand and take them out. No one could safely attack anyone, but no one could leave, either.

"Well, well, well. And we're not even in Mexico," Beatrix said. "You looking to make a deal, Solo?"

"I'm listening," he said.

"No one paid me for you. I'm willing to let you run along your merry way if you want, no strings attached. Just walk away and call it a night. You can tell your grandkids all about it someday."

"Generous," Shane said.

"No," Cassius said immediately over him. "No one leaves."

"I wasn't talking to you," Beatrix told the ghost.

"You stay," Cassius continued. "Both of you stay and beg me to be quick. Beg me to kill you."

Beatrix laughed a genuine laugh of surprised joy.

"Big Boy, my uncle had a rickety-ass card table with foldable legs that looked more stable than that shank dangling under your wide behind. You need to learn when to be intimidating and when to throw in the towel."

"I'm going to peel your lips from your mouth like pulling leeches from flesh," Cassius told her. She laughed again.

"So, what do you say, Solo? I'm a woman of my word."

"I bet," Shane said.

He had little faith in her honor, not that it mattered. The distant sound of a siren was growing closer, and the louder it grew, the more certain Shane was that it was headed in their direction.

The blaring car alarm had disturbed the neighbors enough that someone had called the police. With the deaths at the factories nearby, they'd be more than vigilant about investigating disturbances in the area. And when they arrived, they'd find Winston's body in the house. Anyone still on the property would leave it in handcuffs.

"Oh, sounds like last call," Beatrix said. She snapped her fingers and pointed them at Shane. The gunman raised his weapon. He had yet to speak a word, and he would have been simple collateral damage for Cassius, but he still held power for now, thanks to the weapon.

"You're not giving up already, are you?" Shane said.

"Never, Solo. But I'm not keen on a prison stint. You should have taken my deal when you had the chance."

Shane grunted and watched the gunman warily as he stepped farther from the house. His car was out of commission, but he still needed to flee somewhere, and soon. From the sound of things, the police would be there in a minute or two.

Beatrix began backing away and Shane followed suit, keeping her in view along with Cassius. The ghost did not remain still, either. He used an arm to brace himself and walked purposefully from the house, balancing on the broken limb but keeping most of his weight on the good leg until he was back in the driveway.

"I will kill you both," Cassius said, his statement a matter-of-fact utterance. "It will hurt."

"Sweet talker," Beatrix said, reaching her vehicle and getting inside.

Shane watched as she lifted the lead-lined box from the passenger seat before the gunman circled, got in, and sat there. Shane had a moment of childish satisfaction when he realized the man probably just sat in shards of broken glass.

"I'll be seeing you," Beatrix said. She clapped the box shut and Cassius vanished, sealed within. The engine started, and the vehicle pulled out quickly, leaving Shane alone.

Shane's options were limited. He could run, but he might not get far if there was a large police presence. Instead, he ran to the car the Harvesters had left behind. It was a black luxury car, not the sort of thing that seemed suited to hunting ghosts or killing men, but it would do. The driver had left the keys and a bottle of mineral water in the center console.

August appeared as Shane got behind the wheel.

"Whose car is this?" the ghost asked.

"Who cares?" Shane replied, starting the engine.

August was inside in a blink, and Shane pulled out of the driveway. He stopped at his car and retrieved August's silver dollar before leaving again, heading away from Winston's house and the approaching police as calmly as he could.

He took the first turn he found and then continued weaving through the neighborhood, taking rights and lefts to distance himself from the sirens. He drove in no hurry so as not to draw any attention but made sure he got onto a main road so he could leave the area without being seen.

By the time Shane passed a police car, he was a part of the flow of traffic and didn't look suspicious. The car raced past him in the opposite direction, just as it raced past a dozen others. They were safe for now.

With Cassius in Beatrix's hands, there was no reason to stick around Winston's house. The police would be there soon enough, and if a neighbor had called about the car alarms, then there was a chance they saw

Shane and Beatrix fleeing the scene.

Once the police gained entry to the house, things would get decidedly more difficult. With the man's dead body still in the living room, it would be treated as an active crime scene. Shane had left his fingerprints all over during his fight with the deformed ghosts. None of the Harvesters had worn gloves that he could recall, but he didn't want to explain his presence if he didn't have to.

Shane pressed the button on the car dashboard and brought up the phone. He dialed a number quickly as he drove.

"Don't say anything for a minute," he told August as the phone rang.

"Who would I say anything—"

"Hello?" a voice said, cutting him off.

"Agent Ventura," Shane said. There was a pause on the other end.

"Ryan?"

"You know my voice. I'm touched," he replied. He could hear Ventura sigh. The car's audio was very clear.

"Do you know what time it is?" Ventura asked.

Xander Ventura worked with the FBI as a field agent. But he had the rare talent of being able to see ghosts. He couldn't interact with them like Shane could, but he knew they existed and had, in the past, helped Shane out of a serious jam. It was good to have friends with influence sometimes.

"Of course," Shane replied.

"If you're destroying a whole town again, I don't think I can help square that. I'm still on thin ice," Ventura said.

"Nothing as bad as that. I'm in Manchester, New Hampshire. Just leaving, actually. I was at the home of a man named Benedict Winston."

"Okay…"

"He's dead."

There was another pause from Ventura.

"Okay…" he said again.

"Local cops probably just discovered his body, and they're going to discover my fingerprints all over the house soon enough."

"Hold on," Ventura said. There was some shuffling of movement, and Shane suspected he had woken the man and now, he was sitting up in bed. "So, there's a dead man, and you were in his house, and you left evidence behind. I assume he was murdered?"

"Shot," Shane confirmed. "A few days ago."

"But not by you?"

"This isn't a confession," Shane said. "He was dead when I got there."

"And you didn't call it in because…"

"Because Winston collected ghosts, and some ghost hunters killed him to take one of them. The same one who killed a bunch of people at a frozen fish factory, if you hadn't heard about that yet."

"I hadn't," Ventura said. "Ghost hunters killed this guy to get access to a ghost he had in his collection? How is it killing people at a fish store?"

"Factory. Frozen fish factory," Shane clarified. "They let it loose on purpose. To hunt it."

"Who the hell does that?"

"Ghost hunters," Shane said.

"I mean, sure. Okay. You didn't kill anyone, right?"

"Not yet," Shane told him.

"Please don't phrase it like that."

"I tried to catch the ghost, but they got him back and fled when the cops came. So, everyone's still at large. Two of the hunters died in the fish factory. Chewed up in the machines."

"Jesus. Accident?"

"Ghost killed them. Or at least did most of the heavy lifting. He's a mean one. Think he used to be a cannibal, but that was a lifetime ago."

"A cannibal ghost. And people ground up in fish factory machines. And a man who was shot, with your fingerprints in his house. This is a hell of a call for this time of night, Ryan."

"I thought you'd appreciate it more than anyone else I know," he said.

"Yeah. I'll do what I can. How many bodies are we talking about?"

"At least a dozen," Shane said.

"Jesus. Okay, so I could technically say it's a serial killer. I can pull some strings and get on the case. Give me someone to focus on instead of you."

"The two machine corpses ought to give you a start. Plus a woman named Beatrix."

"Last name?" Ventura asked.

"We didn't exchange business cards. Beatrix. She hunts ghosts. Kind of a loudmouth."

"Mouthy person who goes after ghosts? I can't imagine."

Shane grunted but Ventura sighed over the phone.

"It's something, though. If I can get IDs on her associates, we could have something. Were they in the house with the dead man?"

Shane looked at August, who nodded.

"Yeah. Probably left their prints all over. Someone set up shop and had a few drinks in the kitchen, probably over a couple of days."

"With the corpse?"

"Yeah," Shane said. "These people operate a little darker than most."

"Great. Let me make some calls, I'll get moving. Can I call you back at this number?"

"No," Shane said. "I'm calling from one of their cars."

"Name comes up as Scott Phelps. That one of our corpses?"

Shane raised an eyebrow and shrugged.

"No idea. Look into it. I'll text you a couple of plate numbers, for this car and another one, maybe you can find something."

"Will do. In the meantime, try to stay out of murdered people's houses, will you?"

"No promises," Shane said.

"Naturally," Ventura said, ending the call.

Shane continued toward Nashua, looking at the lit-up dashboard.

Scott Phelps. There were only three men with Beatrix. One had been turned into paste, the gunman had fled in her vehicle, and the third was the coward. He had vanished somewhere during the night. He had been in the car when Beatrix gave them their head start on a hunt. The coward could have been Phelps. It was the best lead Shane had.

"Where were you?" Shane asked, putting Phelps and the whole situation from his mind as they approached Nashua.

"What?" August asked.

"When Cassius caught me in the driveway, and then Beatrix showed up. Where did you go?"

"I was hiding," August said. "Back in the house."

Shane sighed. There was nothing to say that he hadn't said to the ghost already. He wasn't expecting August to be fighting alongside him. Shane didn't rely on others to fight for him, but he was hoping August might find a spine somewhere. Not for Shane, just for himself.

"What are we going to do now?" August asked.

"I'm going home to see what I can learn about Beatrix and whoever Scott Phelps is. I don't know what you're going to do."

"I want to help," he said.

Shane glanced at him.

"Then help," he said bluntly.

CHAPTER 17

A SURPRISE PACKAGE

Shane was sitting at his dining room table drinking coffee. It was just before dawn when he got home from Winston's house, and he didn't get much rest. Ventura had gotten back to him very early with information on the license plates that he had texted. Beatrix had been driving a rental, and that was a dead end. The SUV was found abandoned just outside of Manchester. And the agent confirmed the car Shane had stolen was registered to Scott Phelps.

Ventura didn't have much information about Phelps as he had no record. Still, it was a name they could follow up on. Phelps would be their window to Beatrix. If he'd transacted with her to ghost hunt, he had to have a way to contact her.

"What will you do if you find this Beatrix again?" Carl asked.

Carl and Herbert were watching Shane finish his coffee. August sat at the table as well, watching the ghosts watch Shane. The Davis sisters were whispering among themselves and giggling on occasion from the doorway. They focused on August, and Shane guessed they were toying with him because they could see how jittery he was. He left them to it.

"If she was just hunting ghosts, it wouldn't be an issue," Shane said. "But she killed a man. Pretty sure she would kill me, too, when she was done playing around. I don't think she can be trusted to peacefully go on her way."

"You could call the police," August suggested.

Shane raised an eyebrow over his coffee cup.

"We covered this already. She murdered your friend. And she plans to get rid of you, too," Shane said.

"She can go to jail. Forever. Life in prison, isn't that what murderers get?"

"A dozen people died because she let Cassius go for kicks," Shane added.

"It's still murder. Just a different weapon. She can be punished according to the law. That's how it's supposed to be."

He looked from Shane to Carl and Herbert as though hoping for some support. Herbert gave an awkward shrug, but Carl was more direct.

"How things are and how they are supposed to be are not always the same. There is a wide gap between reality and the ideal. This woman hunts spirits and hunts with them. She kills without hesitation. She is a liability," he said.

"You'd kill her?" August asked.

"Without hesitation. Would you not?"

"I'm not a killer," the younger ghost said with a measure of indignance.

"August is a hider," Shane said.

The ghost frowned, focusing on the table rather than looking any of them in the eye.

"I won't be shamed for valuing life. I lost mine; I know the value of it."

"I lost mine as well," Carl pointed out. "I can assure you that some people are better off dead than alive."

"Then where does it end? Everyone kills everyone, and then what? No one's left," August protested. Shane snickered and continued his coffee. He could see that the new ghost was already rubbing Carl the wrong way.

"I assure you, sir, extinction is not in the cards if we extrajudicially end the life of the occasional monster. Humanity has persevered through thousands of years, many of them far more brutal than the current era.

Killing this woman will not hasten the end of days."

"It's wrong, though. We should strive to be better than those we condemn."

Shane set his mug down with a thunk.

"Beatrix shouldn't have killed Winston. Is that what you're saying, August?"

"Of course!"

"And Cassius, should he have killed those dozen people he killed?"

"No. No one should be murdered," the ghost replied.

"But they were. So, what should have happened doesn't matter unless you have a time machine. 'What should have happened' is a waste of time. It's how children think. 'I wish this,' and 'I wish that.' 'Should have' is meaningless. It's spineless hope for people who rage against the sky for making it rain at a barbecue. What good comes from it? What will change if you keep insisting on how things should be compared to how they are?"

"Nothing, but—"

"Jesus, enough with the buts," Shane said, feeling exasperated. "You came to me. You wanted help. What did you think I was going to do? Talk to Cassius and Beatrix? Scold them?"

"No. I want them to stop."

"So, Beatrix goes to prison, charged with releasing a ghost? And Cassius? Does he go, too?"

"He can go back in the box. And no one has to mention ghosts. She shot Mr. Winston in the head with a gun. That was her, not Cassius."

August was as angry as Shane had seen him, more so than when he'd confronted Beatrix. It was the first emotion besides fear that the ghost seemed able to manifest, and it was refreshing to know there was more than just cowardice inside of him, more than a desire to flee from trouble.

"Cassius could be let loose again if we put him back in the box. Beatrix could get paroled. Hell, maybe she doesn't get prosecuted at all because her lawyers blame it on one of her dead partners at the fish factory. Maybe no one gets punished, and they're free to kill again and again and again."

"You're twisting the point and making up scenarios that don't exist," August countered.

"Like saying what should have happened?" Shane asked him. "You're letting Winston's murderer walk free, August. Just think of all the helpless old men she can slaughter with someone like you in her corner. And Cassius? My God. He could wipe out whole neighborhoods thanks to your compassion."

"Don't blame me for them!" August yelled.

The ghost came at Shane in a clumsy attack. Shane wasn't sure if August intended to choke him or push him. It didn't matter, since he was too slow and uncoordinated. Shane stood and caught him by the neck, forcing the ghost to stand with him.

The sisters went silent, and the room grew uncomfortably cold and dark. The house shuddered, and Carl seemed to loom over the table. Even Herbert took on a more menacing stance as the light bled from the walls and welcomed in shadows from all corners.

Shane held August fast, squeezing tightly. Whatever fight was in August vanished as quickly as it had appeared. Shane had wanted the reaction and had provoked him intentionally to see if there was any fire in the ghost. It wasn't a spark that would push him to do what needed to be done in a pinch, but it proved he wasn't totally hopeless.

"There he is," Shane said, grinning at the spirit. "I was starting to doubt you had balls."

August's hands rested on Shane's wrists, but he did not struggle or fight back. He stared at Shane, looking for all the world like a struck dog.

"I'm sorry. I didn't mean to—"

"Shut up, August," Shane said, releasing him. "Of course, you meant to. I meant for you to. You need to accept that sometimes, you need to get your hands dirty."

The house creaked again, and light slowly refilled the room. Even though none of the ghosts of the house moved an inch, their body language and demeanor shifted as well, back to something relaxed and more casual from the imposing and sinister aspect they had all adopted seemingly without thought.

"What just happened?"

It was Eloise who spoke, standing in front of the sisters in the doorway to the kitchen. August was lucky she had not been present for the argument. Eloise was the least likely to hold her tongue. Or her fists.

"Nothing much," Shane said.

She did not look like she believed him, and her eyes narrowed as she glanced over everyone else.

"Someone is here," she said. "They're coming up the driveway now."

Shane headed to the front door to see who was coming and opened it just as a delivery driver was about to knock. The man had a small package in his other hand wrapped in plain brown paper with Shane's address handwritten on it in black marker.

"Shane Ryan?" the delivery person asked.

"Yeah," he replied as the man thrust an electronic pad at him.

"Sign here, please."

Shane scrawled an awkward electronic signature on the pad and then the man handed over the box.

"Where's this from?" he asked.

"No idea. Just scheduled for same-day delivery."

The driver glanced unsurely at the house and then walked quickly back toward where he had left his truck. Shane looked at the package but could find no indication on the outside about where it had come from.

"What is it?" Eloise asked, inspecting the box closely.

"No idea," Shane said. It wasn't much bigger than a tissue box. It was solid, it felt like wood under the paper, and it had some weight to it. He shook it but heard nothing moving inside.

Shane returned to the kitchen and set the package on the table. The ghosts of the house and August watched as he pulled off the brown paper to reveal a familiar box.

August gasped and moved away from the table. The others looked at him strangely, but Carl focused on Shane.

"You know what this is?" Carl asked.

Shane nodded. It was the same box he'd almost had in his grasp the night before. The lead-lined box that Beatrix had left so casually in the passenger seat of her vehicle. The box that housed Cassius.

The lid was closed and latched. The ghost's haunted item was a very old straight razor. But there was no rattle from within the box that made it seem like it was still there. Someone could have padded the inside to secure the razor in place, but Shane suspected that was not the case.

He flipped the latch up and August produced a curious sound, almost a groan.

"What are you doing? He's secure! He's sealed away; why would you open it?"

"She didn't send Cassius here," Shane said.

Shane was less concerned with what Beatrix had actually sent him than the fact she knew where to send it. She had known the car was his, and she knew where he lived. What else did Beatrix know? And how had she come to know these things?

"Be alert, just in case," Shane said to the others. He lifted the lid quickly, letting it thump on the table as it fell back.

The straight razor was not inside. Instead, there was a single piece of paper, the sort that came from a small notepad. It was folded twice and rested on the bottom of the box.

Shane retrieved the paper and unfolded it. He read the simple, handwritten note and then placed it on the table where the others could see it.

Just wanted to thank you for the fun night, Solo. You're a blast. I'll

126

be by soon to collect what's mine - B.

Carl read it out loud for the benefit of the others and then looked at Shane with a dour expression.

"What's hers?" he asked.

"That one," Shane said, gesturing at August. "She considers him payment for the job she did."

"Payment?" Herbert asked.

"She wants to destroy him to make up for her losses. She seems to think it'll be worth it."

"And you don't want to kill this woman?" Carl asked August.

"I just want this to be over," August said.

"Then we should end it," Shane said. "Come on."

"Where?" the ghost asked.

Shane only had one lead to follow. He didn't want to bring August with him, but he didn't want to leave him at the house, either. Besides, if there was some way to link Cassius to Beatrix, August was the only chance he had of making it. He had to come.

"We're going to see Scott Phelps."

CHAPTER 18

IN THE BLOOD

"Where does this Scott Phelps live?" August asked as they headed down Shane's driveway for the second time.

"Concord. You remember Winston doing business with anyone in Concord?" Shane asked. Concord was just north of Manchester, and the drive would take them less than forty-five minutes. The proximity made Shane suspicious of the arrangement between Phelps and Beatrix if he had indeed hired her as some kind of huntmaster.

He couldn't rule out Phelps being in the dark, though. Beatrix was too knowledgeable. She could have already had a bead on Cassius before Phelps got on board. But if he had initiated the hunt with inside information, then he must have had a significant relationship with Winston.

Shane didn't like so many gaps in the narrative. If he knew enough about all the players and their motives, he could make concrete plans on what to do and how to approach everyone. But there was still too much missing information. Worse, it was a one-sided ignorance. He didn't like that Beatrix knew where he lived.

"Maybe," August said. "I'm sure he'd been to Concord. Remember, he only took me out to shop for food. His other business had little to do with me."

"I know. But think about visitors or phone calls. Anything to do with the name Phelps or Concord."

"Nothing comes to mind," August told him. Shane hadn't expected much more. If there was a situation in which they needed to braise some short ribs, he was sure the ghost would come in handy. But aside from that, he was really dead weight.

Ventura had provided Phelps' address and also kindly had Shane's car towed from outside of Winston's house and impounded in Nashua until he went to pay the bill, so Shane was still driving the stolen car. The windows had a heavy enough tint that it was ideal for being inconspicuous, which, in turn, allowed Shane to scout Phelps' house.

"Won't he notice his car parked outside?" August asked as they approached the man's home.

Phelps had money based on the neighborhood in which he lived. His property had a horseshoe driveway and an elaborately landscaped front lawn. It dwarfed the house on Berkley Street with its vast gardens, well-cultivated trees, and shrub-lined fences.

To the side of the house was a four-car garage, and a red Aston Martin was parked in a small lot out front.

"We just passed four other black Lexuses with tinted windows," Shane said as he pulled to the side of the road on the opposite side where he had a good view of Phelps' house. "I don't think he will notice this one unless he looks at the plates."

They waited and watched the house. August grew restless within the first hour, and Shane made him go for a walk just so he could sit in silence for a bit. Nothing happened at the house, and nothing happened during the subsequent hour, either.

A vehicle eventually pulled into the driveway. It was another black luxury car though Shane couldn't identify the make, and two children in matching uniforms got out. The boy looked to be about ten and the girl might have been twelve. Both wore backpacks and headed to the door as the car left.

"He has kids," August said. "Why would someone with children get involved in something so dangerous?"

"Probably didn't think it was dangerous until it was. He ran off, don't forget," Shane told him.

"If Cassius comes after him…"

The ghost didn't finish the thought, nor did he need to. They stayed in the car, and a half-hour later, another vehicle pulled in. This one parked, and a woman got out. She took a bag from the trunk and headed into the house, talking on a cell phone the entire time.

"His wife?" August speculated.

"Looks like," Shane agreed. "She and the kids look stressed to you?"

"Not really," the ghost answered.

"No. Means Dad isn't missing. Probably right where they expected him to be. He made it home last night. Probably ditched the car so Beatrix wouldn't realize he had taken off until it was too late. But she knows where he lives, and he knows that. He'll be working a deal to save his ass. Might just be a bigger payoff. Looks like the kind of guy who can afford it. But I doubt their business is finished. She'll eventually be paying him a visit."

They sat in silence for another minute, watching the house for any sign of Scott Phelps.

"You do this a lot?" August asked suddenly.

"Stake out rich idiots?"

"Yeah. Track people. Figure out what they're up to and why. You're good at it," he said.

Shane shrugged, noticing movement in one of the windows of the house.

"Maybe. Maybe everything I just guessed is dead wrong, and Phelps is a corpse on his bedroom floor and mom and the kids just walked in on him. Just going with my gut."

"I could never do that. I don't mean to be a coward, you know. I never wanted to be weak."

"No one does," Shane said. "But sometimes, you need to push back. Bend too much, and you'll break."

"Yeah," the ghost agreed. "It's hard to shake it, though. The memory of dying. Being murdered. When I feel like things are getting heated again, it takes me right back to that moment, and I freeze up. I need to get away."

"I get it," Shane said. He had not turned away from the house. "But you need to remember that there's a major difference between that moment and every other one that's popped up since then."

"What's that?" August asked.

"You were alive for the first one."

The door to the house opened, and the children emerged, no longer in uniforms. They piled into the car their mother had been driving, and she joined them. The three left the property and headed right, passing Shane and August without even looking their way.

Shane waited until their vehicle was out of sight, then pulled out of his space, and headed up the drive to Phelps' house, parking in front of the garage.

"What if he's home?" August asked.

"Seems unlikely. Haven't seen a sign of movement before the children arrived. If he is, then so much the better."

"Should I look around first?" August asked as Shane got out of the car.

"There's no point if he can see ghosts. Better to go in together," Shane suggested. No need to let August stumble through and tip Phelps off that something was happening.

Shane had August unlock the door, and then they went inside. The interior of the house further showed off Phelps' wealth. It was a spacious home, and the man had nice things, but there was nothing unusual. He and his wife made a good living, and they provided a nice home for their family. Shane could see nothing suspicious about any of it.

They wandered past family photos and the sort of decorations that people pick up at places like Neiman Marcus and Pottery Barn. There was an abstract mural in the living room above a massive, wall-mounted television.

The kitchen had a breakfast nook, and Shane noticed a temperature-controlled wine cellar next to the fridge that held at least sixty bottles of various vintages. The cat had a bubbler for its water, and it watched August with wide-eyed interest as he walked through.

"This guy doesn't live like a villain," the ghost remarked, looking at a series of baking cookbooks on a shelf near the stove.

"I don't think he's a villain. He might be an asshole, though," Shane said.

Scott Phelps didn't need to live in a dungeon full of body parts to make bad decisions. They continued past the kitchen down a hall. The bathroom was unremarkable, not that Shane expected anything else, but the room across from it was locked. He had August open it and then they ventured inside.

"Wow," the ghost said, taking in the full experience of the space.

They entered a large office that must have belonged to Phelps. The man fancied himself a hunter if the many trophies on display were any indication. He had mounted heads from a dozen species on his wall. There were rams and antelope and even a rhino head, an extremely large buck, a moose, and an elk.

"He likes to kill," August said.

"Some people do," Shane agreed. "It's usually a bit easier when the thing you're hunting isn't trying to kill you and has no idea you're there."

The variety of trophies was enough to confirm for Shane the kind of man Scott Phelps was and why he was with Beatrix. How he had learned about her wasn't relevant, but hunting a ghost made sense now. He must have thought it would have been an amazing thrill without pondering the logistics of how he would hunt a ghost and how dangerous it might be. Cassius was a bold choice.

"I don't understand what he was thinking," August said then, and Shane almost laughed.

"No?"

"He's a trophy hunter. What trophy would a ghost provide? He can't mount Cassius on a wall."

"No, he can't," Shane said. "But he could put a shattered, old, straight razor on display. No one else would know what it was, but he would."

It seemed to click for August then. That was why Beatrix and the Harvesters had taken the other haunted items even after they'd destroyed Winston's ghosts. The haunted item was the trophy. The fact it was broken was proof that the ghost had been caught and destroyed.

It was an obscure trophy. The only way someone would be able to appreciate it would be if they were in on the hunt. People like the Harvesters, or Phelps, who knew about it and were willing to go along with it. It made Shane wonder just how big a community he might be dealing with.

Shane approached a desk near the far wall of the office, ignoring the various trophy heads and other paraphernalia. Phelps had set up a television with gaming systems, a bar, and even a collection of small, boxed bobblehead toys.

Phelps kept very little of importance in his desk drawers. He had typical office supplies and junk in one, and another had unfiled paperwork that Shane rifled through in the hopes of finding something relevant. The odds of Beatrix creating proper invoices seemed slim, but there was a chance Phelps had written something down.

The lights in the office flickered, and Shane paused what he was doing to look up. August said nothing and Shane remained frozen in place, halfway through a stack of Phelps' messy papers. The lights flickered again, and Shane felt a tingle along his arms as the temperature dropped.

"Shane," August said quietly.

He didn't reply because he didn't need to. He could see the shadow rising along the far wall of the office, swallowing the light as the room grew colder. Shane let go of the papers and stood, waiting behind the desk for the ghost that approached.

The floorboards creaked as though someone were walking toward them, but there was nothing to be seen. The shadow spread, and the room became as dark as though the sun had set.

"You don't belong here," a voice whispered. It came from the shadow, but nowhere specific. Shane could not pinpoint the ghost.

"No?" he replied. "Then make me leave."

CHAPTER 19
LIKE FATHER, LIKE SON

The walls shuddered, and the darkness seemed to close in from all around. Shane waited, letting the ghost put on its little show. Finally, the shadows began to coalesce, and the ghost pulled itself together from the darkness.

A man stood before the desk glaring at Shane. He was older, probably in his seventies when he died. He'd lost most of his hair, and his face was heavily lined. His skin was spotty in a way that made it look like he had spent too much time in the sun when he was younger. Shane could see no obvious signs of trauma. However he had died, it had not been violent.

"Leave now," the ghost said, his voice deep and stern.

Shane narrowed his eyes and then reached into his pocket and pulled out a pack of cigarettes.

"Not done yet," he said, retrieving a stick and placing it between his lips. He could see the anger building in the ghost's expression as he raised his lighter and ignited it. Still, the spirit hadn't made a move beyond where he had manifested.

"Who are you?" the ghost demanded.

"Who are you?" Shane countered.

"You come into my house and question me?"

Shane inhaled deeply and then paused before blowing smoke in the ghost's direction.

"Let's not get carried away. You're dead; you're not a property owner."

"I bought this house. I raised my family here!" the spirit insisted.

Shane shrugged.

"So, you're the ex-owner. I'm looking for the current owner. Scott Phelps. Seen him?"

The air stirred, and Shane watched the wisp of smoke rising from his cigarette spin and come apart as the chill in the room deepened.

"Who are you?" the ghost asked again.

Shane nodded, looking the ghost up and down. He was very old, but there was something familiar about him. The shape of the eyes and the nose. He looked like the coward, like Phelps.

"You're his old man," Shane said. "Father Phelps."

"Don't think I can't make you leave," the ghost told him.

"It'd be harder than you think," August piped up.

Phelps had paid little attention to the other ghost until then. Now, drawing his attention, he regarded August for the first time. He was unable to keep his expression even enough to hide his surprise at August's appearance. He didn't seem used to seeing ghosts who died traumatically.

"What do you want with my son?" Phelps asked.

Shane stepped away from the desk and approached a shelf on the wall. Among the trophies and various certificates and knickknacks that the younger Phelps had set up to honor himself were a handful of framed photos. One was of him and the older Phelps, posed together over a deer one of them had shot. Both held rifles, smiling wide for the camera over the corpse below them. It looked to have been taken when the son was maybe in his early twenties, and the senior looked much more vibrant than his spirit seemed to be.

"You hunted together," Shane said.

"What of it?" the ghost replied as though sharing even obvious information was some sort of betrayal.

"Did you get him into it? Bonding experience and all that?"

"I took him hunting as a boy," the ghost said. "Just like my father did for me. It's a character builder. Teaches a man patience and discipline. Teaches respect for life."

Shane laughed and glanced back at August.

"There you go. What you saw when they shot your friend in the head was respect for life. Who knew?"

"Who was shot?" the ghost demanded.

Shane left the photos and returned to the desk, sitting on the edge of it.

"Just one person was shot. Two were dumped into fish processing machines and turned into human smoothies. Though one of them was shot after that. A few were frozen to death with liquid nitrogen. There are six more I'm not sure about just yet, but I'm willing to bet their ends were ugly, too."

"If you're suggesting my son had something to do with that—"

"No," Shane said, cutting the ghost off. "Not suggesting or insinuating or assuming. I'm saying it. He was there. I saw him."

"Scott is no murderer," the ghost said firmly.

"He didn't technically murder anyone," August agreed. "Not with his own hands."

"No," Shane said, inhaling again and holding the smoke briefly. "He just hired the murderers and traveled around with them as they murdered. Legally, there's a huge difference there, right?"

The elder Phelps' veneer of sternness began to waver.

"They killed people?" the ghost said. The confidence had all but drained from his voice.

"They? You know who 'they' are?"

"Scott called them the Harvesters," the ghost said. "He was going to go with them. On a hunt, he told me."

"You could say that," Shane said. "Haven't talked to him since last night then, I take it."

"No," the ghost said. "He came home late, but he didn't come in here. He doesn't like me to leave this room in case the children see. But he didn't come in. I didn't think anything of it. What did he get himself involved in?"

"Just what I told you," Shane said. "Murder. Twelve of them, last I heard."

The ghost turned away from Shane, and the shadows loomed long in the room once again.

"It wasn't supposed to be like that."

He spoke without turning back to face Shane, his voice lower now.

"Never is," Shane said.

"I told him he needed to be careful. He needed to vet these people. You wouldn't go onto the savanna with an untested guide. This was no different."

"You knew he was going to hunt a ghost?" August asked.

"Of course. We talk often. He's my son."

"You're a ghost," August said. Phelps turned to look at him.

"So?"

"So, what if they decide to hunt you?"

Phelps shook his head.

"No, it's not like that. These Harvesters cater to high-profile clientele. Expertly curated hunts. They target wild spirits, lost souls, things that are dangerous to the living. I'm not like that."

Shane laughed, taking the cigarette from his mouth so it wouldn't fall.

"*Wild* spirits? Who sold you that line of BS? The hell is a wild spirit? And what's that make you? Domesticated?"

Phelps glowered and shook his head.

"I'm a man, for God's sake. Like your friend here. They don't hunt men, they hunt… things. Basically animals."

"Do they?" Shane said. He looked at August. "You're an animal now apparently. This has been an informative trip."

Phelps didn't understand the point Shane was trying to make. Whatever his son had told him, or whatever Beatrix had told his son, did not mesh with the reality of how the Harvesters worked.

"They're hunting me. They killed my friends. I'm just a chef. One was a pianist. Another played chess. An actor. We're not animals."

Phelps Senior kept shaking his head.

"No. I told Scott to do his research. These people conduct hunts. It's game hunting. It's like culling, it's not hurting anyone."

"Hate to kill the feel-good spirit, Dad, but there's no such thing as game ghosts or wild spirits or lost souls or whatever. You're all the same. Some are more deserving of destruction than others, don't get me wrong. But this is not a game hunt. They destroy ghosts. If someone paid them, they'd come for *you*, don't doubt it."

"That's not what it was supposed to be," Phelps insisted. "My son is a hunter. He's a sportsman. He's not some vigilante or mercenary."

"Well, he's an accessory to murder now," Shane said. "If it helps at all, it was pretty clear he didn't want to be. From the looks of things, he ran the first chance he got."

"Good. That's good!"

"Maybe. Unless the Harvesters haven't been paid yet, in which case, I expect they will be looking to collect. The woman who runs the outfit isn't the nicest person I've encountered. Not to mention the ghost your son chose."

"What ghost?" Phelps asked.

"Did you know Benedict Winston?" August asked.

"No," Phelps said. "Is he part of this?"

Shane grunted. If Phelps didn't know who Winston was, then he didn't know Cassius. That meant Beatrix was the source of the info on that one. Another thing she shouldn't have known about but did. Just like Shane's address.

Someone else was involved. Beatrix wasn't getting information out of thin air. Someone was feeding her the information she used, and they were well-connected. As old as Cassius was, and as long as he had been imprisoned by Winston, Beatrix's information source had to be much older than her.

"He was my friend," August said to the other ghost. "The people your son had hired broke into his house and shot him in the head. They destroyed my friends and would have destroyed me if I hadn't run. And then they let a monster loose."

Shane finished his cigarette while Phelps' face ran the gamut of emotions. He looked like part of him didn't want to believe what Shane and August were telling him, but mostly, he appeared frightened and maybe even angry.

"You have to believe me. I don't know what you're talking about. Scott wanted to hunt. He found these people, and they looked so professional. There was a whole explanation, a breakdown of the process, costs, and method. It was set up like a real safari. He didn't know anything about any monster…"

"Cassius," August said. "His name is Cassius."

Phelps shook his head, lost in the conversation, while Shane pinched off the cigarette butt, fieldstripped it, and tucked the remains into his jeans pocket.

"He's a killer. Locked away safe and sound since the sixties or so. Then, these Harvesters dumped him in a residential neighborhood down in Manchester. That's where eleven of those twelve dead bodies came from. The hunt didn't go as planned," Shane explained.

"It wasn't supposed to be like that," Phelps said quietly.

"You and he would get along great," Shane said, gesturing toward August with an extended thumb. "Always lamenting how things should have been instead of how they are."

"Is my son safe?" Phelps asked, ignoring the comment. "Are these people going to hurt him?"

"I suppose it depends on Beatrix's mood," Shane said.

Phelps fixed him with a stern glare and hesitated before speaking.

"I lied before. I spoke to him today. He's supposed to be meeting them. He told me the hunt wasn't over. There was a technical hiccup, but he was going back to it tonight."

Shane had not expected to hear that. From the way the younger Phelps had looked the previous night, he was positive that the man would never go back to the Harvesters. He had run away from them. Unless that somehow wasn't what happened. Had Shane misread the situation?

There was no doubt in his mind that Scott Phelps had gotten in over his head. Maybe he just needed a breather to wrap his head around what he was going to do. Why else would he have told his dad he was going back to it?

"Your son watched two people get mulched to a pulp last night. And the ghost that did it will not hesitate to do the same to him if he's foolish enough to go after it again," Shane warned.

"And what will you do if you find my son?" the ghost asked.

"I don't care about your son," Shane told him. "I want to stop the ghost he's after before it kills more people. And I'd like to make sure these Harvesters can't do any of this again."

"You'll let Scott go free?"

"As far as I can tell, your son's just an idiot that got caught up in all this, Phelps. He's free to go on being an idiot. I don't have any beef with him."

The ghost did not look as though he appreciated Shane's commentary, but he was able to see a better deal than what he'd get from Cassius. Phelps didn't want his son to die for making a bad choice.

"He's going to Castor Cemetery tonight. It's down by Bear Brook. He said that's where they're going to hunt this spirit."

Shane knew Bear Brook but not the cemetery. It would be easy enough to find, though. How many cemeteries had ghost hunts going on in small-town New Hampshire?

"He's not a bad person," Phelps said. "No matter what you think, he's not a bad man. He never would have hurt people on purpose."

"He didn't have to go back," Shane said.

He walked out on the ghost without waiting for August. They had plenty of daylight to find Castor Cemetery and set up something before the Harvesters arrived.

He wouldn't go out of his way to harm Phelps, but he had no plans to go out of his way to save the man, either.

CHAPTER 20

WHERE THE DEAD WAIT

Bear Brook State Park was only twenty minutes from Concord, but it was in the thick of rural New Hampshire. The land was all wilderness, the sort of place families went to for a weekend getaway with the kids because it was still just twenty minutes from the nearest McDonald's.

Castor Cemetery was ten minutes from the park, near a blink-and-miss-it town called Barreton. The cemetery was just beyond the town limits on a stretch of road barely wide enough for two cars abreast.

The wrought-iron gates were rusted open and overgrown with weeds. No one had closed them in years, maybe decades. The grounds were not as poorly kept as Shane would have guessed, nor were they particularly pristine. It looked like someone mowed the lawn every month or two, and that was it.

There was a church not far from the cemetery, but the grounds were not connected, and there was no sign that anyone or any place oversaw Castor Cemetery in an official capacity.

There was no parking lot at the cemetery. If someone wanted to visit, they would have to pull off to the shoulder of the road. There was a large enough patch of dirt where a car, maybe two, could park, otherwise one would have to go further up the road or park on the opposite side.

Shane saw no sign of the Harvesters or Phelps, not that he expected them to be there. They seemed to enjoy hunting at night, as though darkness added to the overall experience of going after a ghost. It was a bit theatrical, but they were selling an experience to Phelps, so it probably made sense in that regard.

Shane saw two ghosts in the cemetery. One was an elderly woman who stood in place with her head down; the other was a younger man who strolled between tombstones in no particular hurry. Both looked like they had come from some decades in the past and were probably just regulars, trapped in their routine of wandering and doing little else in the years since they'd died.

Most of the tombstones there were average and unobtrusive. From the road, Shane saw a handful of mausoleums in the distance, near the back of the cemetery. A few monuments also rose above the rest, big stone towers with elaborate decorations or carvings that didn't fit in with the rest of the cemetery. In Shane's experience, that was par for the course. There were always a few people who wanted to stand out from the crowd. In all, it was a very unremarkable cemetery.

"No one's here," August said.

"No, not yet," Shane said. "Gives us time to get the lay of the land."

Shane drove past the cemetery in both directions before deciding to hide the car about five hundred yards from the entrance, behind a gate in a farmer's field. He was forced to break the lock and move the gate out of his way so he could drive the car up what looked like a path for a tractor and hide it behind some overgrowth not far from the road.

Shane and August walked back to the cemetery in the heat of a bright sun and a cloudless sky. It was relaxing to listen to wild birds and trilling insects.

"This is nice," August observed when they reached the cemetery. "Quiet. Looks like people don't come here much."

"Yeah," Shane agreed.

"I could stay in a place like this. I mean, now that Mr. Winston is gone."

"You don't want to be someone else's chef?" Shane asked. The ghost shook his head.

"I don't think I ever should have been there. He was my friend, but I don't know if I was his, if that makes sense."

"It does," Shane said.

He wasn't certain that August understood the nature of the relationship he had with Winston until he'd just said that. As much as he said that the dead man was his friend, it seemed very much to Shane like he was little more than a tool for Winston to use. He wouldn't go so far as to use the word slave, but Winston had definitely used the ghost.

"Do you think you'll kill the Harvesters? If you can?" August asked.

"Maybe," Shane replied.

Planning to kill people was not something he liked to do all that often. Sometimes, some people deserved to die, and sometimes, Shane was the one who made sure it happened. But he was no assassin. He wasn't plotting their murder in the back of his mind. His chief concern was Cassius. He planned to destroy the ghost, and if that ended things, he was happy to leave it there.

But maybe he was kidding himself. On some level, he knew he couldn't just let Beatrix go by telling her not to cause trouble again. She wouldn't listen to Shane. If he got through the night alive and destroyed Cassius, Beatrix would be a problem.

Sending the package to Shane's house was a threat. It was a message telling him that she knew who he was, where he was, and that she would come for him. The easiest thing would probably be to deal with her as soon as he could. Judging from his experiences so far, that would mean only one of them was going to walk away.

He had trouble admitting it, but he was hesitant to kill Beatrix. He didn't know her, and she didn't owe him anything. She had been nothing but trouble so far, and he doubted she would hesitate to kill him. But she was also like Shane. She could do the things Shane could, and that was unusual.

Shane was probably just feeling a bit of misplaced sentimentality. There was no bond of brotherhood just because they could both break a ghost's jaw. He could make peace with the idea that she was a problem that needed to be solved, even if she was like him in terms of what she could do. If it came down to a fight, he would not hesitate. She'd done nothing to earn his mercy.

They reached the gates of Castor Cemetery and entered like any other visitor. Shane walked through the rows of tombstones, glancing at each on the way past. Many of the dates were from the forties, and the most recent were from the eighties and early nineties, though he did find one that was only five years old.

There was one recently dug grave not far from a small tree at the western edge of the cemetery, but nothing marked who it might belong to. It was out of place given the state of the rest, but no spirits were nearby, and nothing was out of the ordinary about it other than being fresh and open.

The mausoleums at the rear of the cemetery dated back to the twenties, though the ones interred could have been more recent since they were family plots. Some parts of the grounds were so overgrown that smaller tombstones were obscured behind grass and weeds. Maintenance was no one's priority at Castor, possibly part of the reason why the Harvesters had chosen it. It didn't seem like people went there often.

Aside from a handful of trees and the mausoleums, the cemetery did not offer much in the line of cover or hiding places. Someone low to the ground could have gone unseen, particularly at night if it was only human eyes looking for them. Ghosts and the Harvester's thermal cameras would have made short work of anyone trying to go unnoticed.

As Shane and August walked the cemetery, they ran across several more spirits. It was far from the most active cemeteries Shane had been in, but it had a decent number of the dead wandering free and minding their own business. That could have been another part of the motivation for choosing it as a hunting ground, Shane realized. The ghosts already there would throw off the thermal cameras enough to make it at least a partial challenge.

"Have you seen anyone poking around here lately? People using technology, or new ghosts?" Shane asked, approaching an elderly woman's ghost.

She stood over a grave that Shane had at first assumed was hers. But the name etched into the plain, gray slab was Evan Harlow, and the dates showed he'd been dead for more than seventy years. He died when he was only four. The epitaph was simply "Beloved son."

The ghost lifted her head. She wore a long, elegant black dress with lace along the sleeves and a design across the bodice that could only be seen when the light hit it just right. Her flesh was as white as milk, and it hung loosely from her as though it had been pulled over her skull and left like that.

Cloudy, brown eyes regarded Shane with interest, and the ghost's expression was grim as she scanned his face.

"I see you," she said quietly.

"And before me?" Shane asked.

"A hundred men. All dead now. A hundred before that. A hundred more tomorrow. Maybe you, too," she told him.

"One day," Shane smiled. "But not tomorrow. We're looking for hunters, people who can see ghosts. Hunt ghosts. Anyone like that been through here?"

The ghost made a sound like a growl in her throat, a wet crackle as though she were calmly clearing it. She squinted and her mouth pulled thin.

"The woman. With the shaved hair," the ghost said.

"That's the one."

"You should leave. You're not wanted here."

Her expression darkened and her voice lowered, taking on a more masculine register that was tinged with anger.

"I'm not with her. I'm looking for her."

"She's not wanted here, either. She's done enough. Go while you can.

No one here has forgotten her."

"We're trying to stop her," August piped up. "She killed a friend of mine, and—"

"You are not wanted here," the ghost hissed, cutting him off. "If you bring her here, you will be punished."

"She's coming here with or without us," Shane said. "She'll be here soon. If you don't want her doing whatever she did last time, you should tell me what you know, and maybe we can work together."

The ghost moved in a way Shane had never seen. She was standing before him, looking him in the eye and talking to him, and then she just wasn't. Suddenly, she was at his side, her cold hand on the back of his neck, and her ragged, sharp nails were pressed against his throat.

"Whatever she did?" the ghost hissed. Her lips were at his ear, and when she spoke, Shane could smell rose and jasmine and something citrusy on top of something rotten, like someone had perfumed a dead body. "She took him."

Her nails dug into Shane's jaw, and she forced his head down to look at the grave she had stood at.

"She broke him like he was a piece of glass, and he was no more," the ghost whispered in his ear. "We were going to be together forever. It was my reward. So many years without him. I thought I'd lost him, but he was here waiting for me. And then she took him!"

"And she's coming back," Shane said calmly. "So, what are you going to do about it?"

He felt the ghost's hand tense, the fingers growing more rigid as they started to dig into his flesh, but she relented a moment later. The cold hand suddenly fell away and she was back where she had been, looking down at the grave of her lost child.

"Nothing," she said, no longer looking at Shane.

"Nothing?" August asked, not understanding her.

"Nothing," she said again. "She took everything I had. What should I

148

do now? Let her take me as well?"

She looked up at August, and there was no anger on her face this time, only anguish. A deep sadness Shane had not seen in a very long time.

"She enjoyed it. It gave her joy to take my boy from me; I could see it in her eyes. I will not give her that joy again. I would rather spend eternity alone than give her that gift."

"When was she here? When did she take your son?" Shane asked.

The ghost shook her head dismissively as though the question didn't matter.

"Years. I don't pay attention to these things anymore."

"Was it the only time she's been here?"

"No. Once before. She was much younger then. She claimed the old man with the broken face from the mausoleum that time. She comes and takes. And if she comes again, she'll take again. She can kill us," the ghost answered, speaking to August. "She can end you."

"She wants to," August said, "but I have to stop her. We do."

He gave Shane an awkward look, but the elderly ghost didn't notice.

"Kill her. Shoot her or stab her. Hit her with your vehicle. Cave in her skull and leave her for the insects. But do it quickly, before she can fight back. It's all she deserves," she said and then vanished.

Her advice wasn't bad. It sounded like Beatrix had been the way she was for years, and that nothing would stop her anytime soon.

"Come on," Shane said to August. "We need to get out of sight before they arrive."

Chapter 21
SHOWDOWN

The sun was setting, and darkness was encroaching on Castor Cemetery. There were no lights in the vicinity, and the sky was partially cloudy. Shane would have the scant light from a half-moon to guide him once the sun was gone.

They were across the street from the cemetery, hidden in a field behind a boulder next to a wall of vines that had grown over a wire fence. Shane had a fairly clear view of the cemetery, but because he was not on the grounds, he hoped that his presence would go unnoticed by the Harvesters when they arrived. He hoped the rock would mask his heat signature if they scanned in his direction.

August and Shane had covered the grounds of the cemetery well enough to have a general idea of the layout. There would be no surprises once Shane got in there in search of Cassius and Beatrix. Now, all he had to do was wait for the Harvesters to arrive to start their hunt.

August was blessedly quiet for the most part, having little to say after their cemetery tour. It was clear he felt very conflicted about everything that had happened to him. Shane was comfortable letting him work out his inner turmoil all on his own.

Darkness crept over everything as the sun vanished beyond the horizon, and night came into its own. The half-moon gave some ambient light, but there was nothing to see. No cars had come down the road in more than an hour, and none had stopped anywhere near the cemetery. The Harvesters and Phelps were not there.

Nearly an hour had passed in full darkness, and Shane was beginning to think that the elder Phelps had either led him astray or just had the wrong information. Maybe something had happened elsewhere with Cassius, or maybe Beatrix had switched plans so that Phelps wouldn't be able to alert someone if he had a change of heart. There were a hundred possible explanations, but none of them let Shane know what was going on. He was in the dark looking at an empty cemetery.

The idea of calling it had crossed Shane's mind more than once. He could go back to Phelps' house and get some more information from the ghost, or even Phelps' wife. Maybe Phelps had a computer that he did business on and had used to communicate with the Harvesters. The trail wasn't dead yet.

As Shane pondered potential next steps, August placed a hand on his shoulder, shaking him excitedly.

"There," the ghost said, pointing into the dark cemetery.

It took Shane's eyes longer to adjust and to make out what August saw with his enhanced vision. A figure was walking through the tombstones. Not Beatrix or the gunman or Phelps, not someone alive at all. It was Cassius.

Shane scanned the cemetery. He saw no sign of the Harvesters or a vehicle.

"Do you see the others?" Shane asked.

"No one," the ghost said.

"Where did he come from?"

"He was just there," August said. "I didn't notice him until now."

"Maybe they're on the way," Shane said.

He rose from behind the boulder and hopped the fence. August came with him, almost questioning what he was doing but then thinking better of it as he ran across the street after Shane and then through the open wrought-iron gates.

Despite the injury he had sustained at Shane's hands, Cassius was still able to walk. He was slower now and limping significantly, but he balanced his leg in a way that kept him upright and mobile. Shane regretted not making it more severe when he had the chance.

He had envisioned doing things differently. If the Harvesters had shown up like he planned, released Cassius, and then went on a hunt for him afterward, Shane would have just swooped in and taken the lead-lined box. If he had the ghost in his possession, he could deal with it where he wanted and when he wanted without worrying about Beatrix. Things were more complicated now. Still, he could do something without Beatrix and the others interfering, he just needed to move quickly.

The other ghosts in the cemetery paid Cassius little mind, and he returned the favor. He looked like he was heading somewhere with a purpose as Shane approached from the entrance. If he was still in Beatrix's possession, Shane had no time to plan a crafty attack. It was going to be dirty.

Cassius saw him coming as he entered the cemetery grounds and stopped, smiling behind his mop of greasy hair.

"I was hoping to see you again," the big ghost said.

"Yeah?" Shane replied.

He didn't stop moving as he approached. Instead, he swiftly dropped low and planted an elbow into the side of the ghost's knee. The broken leg gave out, and the ghost fell with a cry of surprise, dropping to his good knee next to Shane.

Cassius made to speak but Shane's fist caught him under the jaw. His mouth snapped shut, and a second punch knocked his head sideways, releasing a tooth that vanished as it flew into the grass.

The ghost roared and lashed out with a big swing, clipping Shane across the face and knocking him onto his back. Cassius pulled at the nearest tombstone and lifted it from the ground, raising the slab of stone above his head as he turned to face Shane.

"I'm going to crush your head into bone meal, and paint this cemetery with the sludge," he growled. "I will—"

Shane's foot was up before Cassius finished the threat. His heel hit the ghost square in the chin, snapping his head back. A second kick took the ghost in the neck, and he dropped the rock to clutch at his throat.

Cassius lashed out again, but Shane scrambled out of range and got back to his feet. He was barely upright when he had to drop to the ground again, avoiding the headstone as it hurled end over end toward him. The slab shattered against another tombstone a short distance away.

As Shane got to his feet, Cassius hurled another stone that he barely avoided.

The ghosts of Castor were paying attention now. Several had gathered, and there were many more than Shane had previously seen. Close to a dozen were in a loose circle around the fight. None spoke or moved to interfere, but their interest made Shane nervous.

Cassius hurled a third stone, and it shattered next to Shane, peppering him with small bits of rock. The ghost was still on one knee and had pulled all the headstones from the ground near him, giving him nothing to use as a weapon until he crawled to the next stone.

Shane ran at him, hoping to stop him from getting his hands on another projectile. A leg slipped out of the shadows and tripped him before he reached Cassius, and he fell forward, barely catching himself before his face smashed to the ground.

One of the ghosts who had been watching jumped on him, fists battering against the back of his head. The ghost fought poorly, unskilled, and barely effective, but the distraction allowed Cassius to reach another large stone.

Shane struggled with the strange new ghost, an older man who looked as though he had drowned, as Cassius pulled the large, wedge-shaped monument out of the earth.

"You lose," he bellowed, holding it over Shane's head.

The death blow never came. Another ghost attacked, this one coming for Cassius and not Shane. A thickly built spirit with massive trauma down the left side of his body tackled Cassius and caused the tombstone to fall harmlessly.

More of the Castor spirits joined, coming for both Shane and Cassius. They shouted angrily, making threats and swearing, but there seemed to be no guiding desire or purpose. They were angry, and they were taking it out on the strangers in their midst, nothing more.

Shane fought off a woman with hair like old straw and broke the arm of the one who had tripped him. Cassius tore the head from the ghost that had attacked him, but more were quick to replace it.

Beyond Cassius, August was running as one of the cemetery ghosts attacked him as well. He called to Shane for help, as though ignorant of Shane's predicament as more spirits piled on.

They came from all sides. There were more than twenty, though Shane had no time to count. Most were typical ghosts, the mundane sort that haunted cemeteries and never aspired to be anything frightening or powerful. They fought the way they would have fought in life, with no skill or plan, just feeding off the mob and hiding behind numbers.

Shane countered where he could with quick, debilitating strikes. He was not looking to destroy anyone; the numbers wouldn't allow him the time. But he could maim, and so he did.

He aimed for knees and elbows. He crushed fingers, punched throats, and broke noses. The influx of spirits throwing punches and kicks was overwhelming, even with his counters. Feet like bricks of ice took him in the ribs and spine. Fingernails raked at his flesh and gouged his cheeks and scalp.

Shane was knocked onto his back and rolled over, pinned by a trio of ghosts as a large man in a tuxedo loomed over him, ready to drop a boot on his face. He struggled free, but more ghosts piled on, holding him steady. The well-dressed spirit said nothing and dropped his foot.

The sound of the ghost grunting came an instant after something hit him hard from the side. The ghost tumbled away, and Shane watched as

Beatrix twisted his head in one smooth motion, pulling it from his body and causing him to explode with enough force to knock away all the ghosts holding Shane down.

He got to his feet quickly while Beatrix matched his pace. They made eye contact but exchanged no words. The ghosts were on them again, and the fight would not be paused.

Shane found himself back-to-back with the woman he had planned to kill a short time earlier.

"Looks like you owe me," she said as she snapped the arm of an old woman and then twisted the ghost's head around.

Shane broke the knee of another and forced it to the ground, bringing his elbow down hard into its back, and then crushing its head. The force knocked the dead back once more but did not scare them off.

"You're still alive. Debt repaid," Shane told her.

Beatrix laughed, a light and giddy sound, and laid into another spirit, catching a punch, and breaking the ghost's fingers before kicking it away.

Some of the ghosts abandoned their efforts to fight Shane and Beatrix and focused instead on Cassius. The monster spirit was already crippled, and they took him for an easier target. He showed them quickly that, if anything, he was more efficient at destruction than Shane and Beatrix. He used his speed and bulk to crush heads with thunderous blows from his fists. The explosive bursts buffeted against Shane again and again like an unseen force.

A crackling of electrical energy sent a handful of spirits reeling. Shane turned to his other side to see Phelps using a device that Shane vaguely recognized from his first encounter with the Harvesters. It looked like a complex remote control but discharged energy that surged through the spirits and knocked them down. They had used the same device on Cassius, but it had not been as effective. The weaker spirits of Castor were much less resilient.

The device served to aid Cassius more than Beatrix or Shane, clearing the big ghost's foes enough for him to get the upper hand and destroy two before the others ran off. After destroying the final spirit, he did not hesitate before coming for Shane and Beatrix.

"He's coming—" Shane began, turning to warn the woman behind him. Her fist hit him hard in the face, a bit too low to break his nose but spot-on to bust his upper lip. He stumbled back, spitting blood.

Beatrix laughed.

CHAPTER 22

DOWN BELOW

Beatrix turned her back on Shane almost immediately and focused on Cassius, working his one good leg with a pair of swift kicks before dodging his counter.

Phelps circled them and hit Cassius with another energy blast from his stun weapon. Cassius and Beatrix traded blows and blocked one another before the ghost opened himself to an impossible to defend strike. He took the hit along his thigh, but it allowed him to redirect and slam the box in Phelps' hands up into the man's face, smashing it against his chin and mouth.

Phelps cried out like an animal. The device shattered and fell to pieces along with a splash of the man's blood. Shane guessed the attack had cost him some teeth, and the shards of the device had badly cut his chin, lips, and nose. He fell to the ground, clutching the wounds, and screaming into his hands.

Shane was not surprised to see Beatrix laughing again. She used the distraction as an opportunity and slashed her hand down on Cassius' face like a wild cat fighting prey. She tore the ghost's ear from his head, and he screamed in rage.

"Help me," Phelps yelled as another of the cemetery ghosts dragged him backward now that he was defenseless.

"Your check cleared, Big Shot. Help yourself," Beatrix shouted back, kicking Cassius in the neck.

Shane fought off another pair of the local spirits, crushing one's skull and forcing the other away with one less arm than when he'd started.

Phelps screamed as a ghost set upon him, attacking like an animal as it clawed at his ruined face. Unlike Shane and Beatrix, Phelps had no defense. He could see spirits, but he could not interact with them. He would be torn to pieces if someone didn't save him.

Shane cursed and bypassed Beatrix, coming to Phelps' aid. He pulled the ghost off him by the head, twisting the spirit's neck until it faced the wrong direction.

"You don't belong out here, Phelps," Shane said, offering him a hand. "You need to—"

The words were clipped off as Shane's mouth snapped shut. Something heavy slammed atop his head from behind, and a flash of light flooded his field of view. The world spun. Shane's body felt light, but it was hard to tell if he was standing or falling or already lying down.

The sounds of the fight died out, and soon, there was just a droning hum. Everything was dark.

Shane knew his eyes were open, but there was nothing to see. He was lying down and tried to sit up. His head hit something flat and hard only inches in front of him, and he fell back, hitting what felt like padded wood with the back of his head.

Pain resonated through his skull. Something had hit him hard in the head. It felt like his skull had busted open, but he could not lift his hand to inspect it. He was in a box, something long and narrow. A coffin.

The air was slightly stale. He could smell dirt, wood, and his sweat. It was warm and humid in the box, and he had only inches of space between himself and the lid. He pushed up with his hands and feet, but the space was too confined to get any leverage. It didn't even shift.

He ran his hand along the edges, feeling for a seam or a gap. Any place he could perhaps wedge his hand to get a grip and move the lid. There was nothing.

Shane began to kick in controlled, short jabs with his foot. His boot hit the coffin lid with a dull thud again and again. Whether he managed to break the wood or get the lid to lift, he didn't care. He needed something to give way.

He found himself yawning as he worked, and his head felt fuzzy. He attributed it to the head wound at first, but the stale smell of the air became hard to ignore. The coffin had been sealed, which meant there was no oxygen. He was breathing in his breath again, the CO2 levels rising with each exhalation.

Shane guessed how much air was in the coffin given its size. He had very little headroom or leg room, and just as little from side to side. If the coffin was airtight, he suspected there was only about twenty minutes of oxygen. But that would have been from the moment he was sealed in, and he was unconscious when that happened.

He began to feel weak and tired. It was hard to stop from yawning and to keep his thoughts straight. He had been unconscious for longer than he'd suspected. Most of the air had already been used. Fatigue from lack of oxygen was setting in, and it was something he knew happened quickly.

Sweat ran down the sides of his face as his mind raced with what else he could do. There had to be some way to crack the wood, to allow air in while he worked to free himself.

He reached into his pocket and felt iron rings and his lighter. The rings would be no help, but the lighter might do something. He pulled the Zippo out awkwardly and raised it to chest height. His hand was nearly pinned, and he had only a few inches to work with.

He held the lighter tightly and flicked open the lid. The coffin was made of wood; he could burn through it.

No. That was a stupid idea. He would waste the last of his oxygen and achieve nothing. If the coffin was buried, the fire wouldn't even get through.

He shook his head. He wasn't thinking straight. He needed to keep focused. He needed to be smart.

Shane scraped the lid of the lighter against the roof of the coffin. It scratched the surface and left a small gouge that he could feel with his finger. He did it again and again.

He got into a rhythm scraping the wood over and over. Up and down, up and down, dragging the sharp corner of the Zippo lid across the wood over his chest. Every so often, he checked it with his finger. He was digging into it, making progress, and had formed a deep gash. But it was only a few inches long. He could never use it to escape.

It didn't matter. He needed air first. He was looking for air, not escape.

He continued scraping. His forearms felt weak even though the effort was minimal. It shouldn't have been so hard. It *wasn't* hard; he was simply losing air.

How long had he been at it? He had not kept track of time. Was it five minutes? Fifteen? He couldn't remember.

The coffin went silent, and he stared at the darkness. He'd stopped scratching and hadn't realized it. He wanted to start again, but he was so tired. Each breath felt thin.

The scratching started again. He would escape. He would survive because he had to. He felt the lighter in his hands, cold and solid. He clutched it in his palm. He was not moving it. It wasn't scratching. The sound was from somewhere else.

"Hello?" Shane said weakly.

The scratching came from outside the coffin. Something was outside. He kicked his foot again, weakly slamming his heel into the bottom of the box. It sounded loud to his ears, and he hoped it was heard outside.

Something loud answered. It was above his face, and he felt a sprinkle of fine dust on his cheeks and lips. Something was outside and *trying to get in.*

"Hey," he said, unable to shout. "Hey!"

He kicked again and again. The scratching and thumping outside continued and then stopped. He waited, his head swimming. Even though he saw nothing but darkness, it swirled in his mind.

Something metal squeaked and wood groaned. Light blazed into Shane's face, and he shut his eyes, turning his head as the lid of the casket was pulled aside.

Cool, fresh air rolled over him, and he breathed deeply, filling his lungs at last with fresh air. He gulped, breathing in heavy gasps until the swimming feeling in his head subsided and he could focus.

A flashlight pointed down at him, and he lifted his hand to shield his eyes. The beam moved aside, and darkness filled the space. He gave his eyes a moment to adjust.

"Sorry," a familiar voice intoned from above.

Shane blinked, trying to focus on who was on the other side of the light. It took a moment to recognize Scott Phelps. The man's face was a mess of blood and cuts, but he was alive.

"We thought you were dead," August said.

The ghost was behind Phelps, at the top of a hole. Shane was in an open grave. He had been sealed in the casket and someone had partially buried him, but only enough to hide the fact a casket was there. Phelps still held the shovel he'd used to unearth the box.

"What the hell happened?" Shane asked, sitting up. It took a moment as a wave of dizziness overcame him. He couldn't say if it was caused by the lack of oxygen or the wound on the back of his head.

"Lanthimos hit you in the head," Phelps explained.

"Who the hell is Lanthimos?" Shane replied.

"The guy with the gun," August answered.

Shane nodded, and even that hurt. He had forgotten about the gunman in the heat of the fight. He'd been so focused on Beatrix and Cassius that he'd overlooked her sidekick.

"And what? They left you here to almost-but-not-quite kill me?" Shane asked as he got to his feet.

"They left me for dead, too," Phelps said. "I was unconscious, and I gather I don't look so good right now."

"This Lanthimos fellow closed the box and recaptured Cassius," August explained. "I don't think they planned on all those other spirits being involved. Beatrix destroyed a few after Cassius was captured, and the others fled. They tossed you into a pine box and then this open grave."

"Where the hell did they get a pine box and an open grave?" Shane asked.

"Both were here already," August said.

Shane recalled seeing the grave on his first pass, but not the box. Beatrix had planned ahead.

He crawled awkwardly from the hole, feeling his head throbbing from the wound he'd sustained. Once back on level ground, he saw that most of the spirits had vanished. It was still night, but Beatrix and Cassius were gone.

Phelps needed help to get back out of the hole. His face looked like raw meat from the nose down. He needed medical attention and probably a good number of stitches. Shane needed some as well. The wound on his head felt raw, and he could feel blood when he gingerly explored it with his fingers. He didn't have time to clean up, though.

He would not let that woman escape again.

CHAPTER 23

HUNTER/HUNTED

"How long ago did they leave?"

"More than an hour ago," Phelps answered.

Shane cursed. An hour could have taken them anywhere. They'd be impossible to track. Phelps was the only lead he had, and it was clear they had cut ties.

With a grunt, Shane leaned back against a large tombstone, supporting himself as he reached into his pocket and pulled out a cigarette. Now that he could breathe again, he felt like a smoke was in order.

"How did you hook up with these people?" he asked as he flicked the Zippo to life.

"I had a friend who had a friend," Phelps said. "I had never even seen a ghost until my dad died. Or I never thought I did. I guess I must have in the past without realizing it."

"Some can do a good job of blending in," Shane agreed, lighting the cigarette.

"But my dad… I was there when he died. I buried him. He was gone. And then he wasn't. I pissed myself when I saw him again. But it was just him. Same as he always was. Better even."

"Better?" August asked.

"My old man never talked about how he felt or what he thought. I know he loved me, and he was always there, but he never said that kind of stuff. But when he came back… it was like a veil had lifted. He talked about everything. He opened up to me. It was incredible."

"So you thought, 'Hey! I should go destroy some ghosts for fun!'"

Shane said.

Phelps shook his head and winced, reaching for his ruined face but stopping short of touching it.

"It wasn't like that. We always hunted together. I looked into ghosts after he came back. I learned about them and found out that some were not like my old man. Some came back bad, like all those horror stories you hear. So, we got to talking, and my old man suggested it. Why not do something about it? I think he was insulted that he was one of them, and some were lowlifes."

"Lowlifes," Shane said, chuckling. "Sure."

"I met people who knew about it. People who would even sell you a ghost if you wanted one. People who hang out with them and have haunted houses on purpose."

"Crazy world," Shane said.

"And then I heard about the Harvesters. It was exactly what I wanted. Ghost hunters. They take you out on a hunt to get rid of a ghost that doesn't deserve to be here. Not ones like my dad or your friend here; bad ones. Evil ones. It was perfect."

"It's not perfect," August said.

"No, I know that now" Phelps agreed. "You have to believe me; I didn't know. They gave me a list of ghosts I could hunt. It was just a description of what they were. This one was just listed as a murderer. Dangerous, smart, and nearby. I never even knew its name. It was the most expensive one they had, but it sounded great. They assured me it'd be safe. We'd track it, catch it, and destroy it. That was how it was supposed to be."

"But you killed Mr. Winston," August said. "And Cassius killed so many others. There was nothing safe about it."

"I never knew about Mr. Winston. I never would have agreed to that. I was shocked when she shot him. I was terrified. I realized this was not what I signed up for, but she threatened me. She threatened my kids. If I didn't stick with her, if I didn't pay and finish the hunt, she'd take her payment out in pain."

"You could have called for help," August said coldly. Phelps scoffed.

"From whom? The police? What was I supposed to tell them? I hired a psychopath to help me hunt a dead man, and now she's murdering people?"

Phelps was an idiot, but he was right. He had painted himself into a corner. No one would have believed his story, and there were too many holes to make up a clever lie. Plus, Beatrix was not the type of person to make idle threats. If his family was thrown into the mix, Shane knew Phelps himself would have pulled the trigger on Winston to keep them safe.

Beatrix had cut Phelps loose when it seemed like his fortune had turned and he was going to die. His family would probably be safe now. Money had changed hands and Beatrix was done with the job. The hunt hadn't played out the way Phelps had wanted it, but she didn't care. She'd gotten what she'd come for, and she still had the ghost. She could destroy him at her leisure if she wanted to.

"How did Beatrix find out about Cassius?" Shane asked.

Phelps shook his head.

"She wasn't transparent about how the business runs. They came to me; I never went to them. I don't know where they're based, how many there are, or anything. They just had a list of about ten ghosts. I picked this one because it was in Manchester. I wouldn't have to be away from home for long to do the hunt."

Shane puffed on the cigarette between his lips and stared at the man.

"This how you always work? I saw your office; you had a rhino head in there. You just fly to Africa and hook up with the first random guy who says he can take you out on the savanna?"

"Of course not," Phelps replied. "But this is different. This is under- underground. No one does this. There's no competition, so it's not like I can vet these people. The fact they even knew what I wanted was confirmation enough that they were the best option and the real deal. I just had no idea they'd be so irresponsible. She got her people killed and didn't bat an eye!"

"I saw," Shane said. "What about the tech? The thermal scanners and your little stun gun. Where's all that from?"

"They showed up with it. Gave me a fifteen-minute lesson in how to use it, and we were ready to go."

"What about her deformed ghosts?"

"The hounds?" Phelps asked. "That was when I ducked out. I didn't see those until the night she sent them after you. I'd never seen anything like them."

"Does she have more?"

"I have no idea. She had Lanthimos open a box. There was some trinket inside, and then this ghost appeared. Like an animal that was once a man. It was a goddamn nightmare."

All questions and no answers. Beatrix didn't let anyone in that she didn't need to. Her business was mobile, and she used rental vehicles and probably fake names. No one knew a damn thing about her, and she knew everything about everyone else. She had a grave dug before Shane arrived; that wasn't a coincidence. That was her banking on needing it.

"So, your point of contact was just a phone number?" Shane asked.

"I got a number from someone an associate knew. Guy who used to trade in ghosts. I called, and from then on, she called me," Phelps explained.

"Probably a burner phone, too. We've got nothing now. Not a damn thing."

"That's not entirely true," Phelps said.

Shane exhaled smoke slowly. He stared the man in the eye and waited for the follow-up.

"After what happened at Mr. Winston's house, I didn't trust her anymore. I mean, who would? She killed a man, she got her people killed, and she threatened my family. I couldn't leave her, but I sure as hell wasn't going to let her leave me, either. I figured she'd pin the murders on me or stiff me on my money or something."

"So...?" Shane said.

Phelps smiled, and the expression made his broken face look even more terrifying. He held up his cell phone.

"I put an AirTag on her SUV."

"An AirTag?" August asked.

Shane smiled and stood, walking over to Phelps, and looking at the screen.

"Tracker. Looks like they're about fifty miles west of us."

Shane watched the screen. From the look of things, Beatrix was not moving. He checked the location on the map, and a name and address came up.

"Motor Court Inn," Shane said quietly. They'd stopped at a cheap motel. Beatrix had survived the fight in better condition than Shane, but she had taken her fair share of hits. She'd need rest.

"Do you have anything else?" Shane asked.

"I recorded our last couple of phone calls, but that's all," Phelps said.

It was better than nothing. Shane was surprised Phelps had the wherewithal to do what he'd done. He wasn't as dumb as he seemed. He was dumb, just not *that* dumb.

"Go home. Gather whatever you have; I might need to send it to a friend. Either way, go get your face fixed before you bleed to death or get some flesh-eating infection," Shane told him.

Phelps raised a hand and touched his mouth again as though he'd forgotten what happened. He winced and nodded.

"You're going after them?" he asked.

"Plan to get this over with tonight," he replied. "I'm keeping your phone."

He pocketed the device, and Phelps looked like he might protest but thought better of it. Shane looked at August, holding the spirit's gaze for just a moment before he nodded.

Phelps watched them leave, heading out of the cemetery toward the gate. The elderly woman's ghost was still there, watching Shane as he passed.

"She escaped," the ghost said.

"No, she didn't," Shane corrected. "Night's not over."

He led August back down the street to where he'd hidden Phelps' car. He realized he'd left the man with no way to leave other than walking. Phelps would probably live long enough to get to the nearest town and get help. It could have been worse.

Phelps' phone synced with his car as Shane started the engine, displaying driving directions to the motel. As they headed out, August turned to look out the window.

"I killed someone," he said softly.

Shane raised an eyebrow, speeding down the empty road toward the nearest highway.

"That so?" he said.

The ghost nodded.

"In the cemetery. He was an old man. He came at me when you were fighting Cassius. He was skinny and short and older than my grandfather. He had a big mole on his head, and I couldn't stop staring at it, even as he strangled me. His hands were on my throat. I could feel him squeezing it, feel it tightening in his grip."

"Ghosts can do a lot of damage to each other," Shane said.

"I felt like I couldn't breathe, but I don't even need to breathe. It made me panic."

"Feeling like you're going to die, even if you aren't really going to die, gets in your head. Makes you lose it sometimes."

"I understand that now. I was so… terrified. I died once already; I know what it's like. And feeling like it might happen again... I lost control."

"You fought back."

"I saw what you'd done. I grabbed his head and just pushed and pulled as hard as I could. I needed him to go away. And his head twisted. It snapped. I fell over with him, and it came off. It pulled right off his body, and then he didn't have a body anymore. He burst like a balloon, and vanished like he never was."

"Head's always a surefire weak spot," Shane agreed. "Hard to exist without one, alive or dead."

"The energy that rushed from him was overwhelming. It felt like when you hit the beach for the first time, and the sun is bright and the air is warm. Just invigorating. I've never felt anything like it. But then I realized what I'd done."

"You defended yourself," Shane said. "No need to feel guilty about it. Guy was already dead, anyway."

"But so am I! How do I deserve to exist more than he did? What right do I have to survive and take the life of another?"

Shane sighed, taking a turn to follow the car's directions.

"You didn't take a life. He had no life. You ended his existence. A small distinction, but relevant. He chose to end yours first; you just prevented him from doing something he had arguably no right to do. His choice forced your choice. Unless you think you deserved to lose that fight just because he wanted to rip you apart."

"No," August said.

"Good. You're not suicidal, then. Everything, living or otherwise, has a right to defend itself from an attacker. You came out on top. Someone had to."

"I suppose you're right," the ghost said.

"I am," Shane confirmed.

August continued to stare out the window as they drove with little else to say. Shane was glad for the rest. He didn't want to continue the conversation, he needed to focus. They would be at the motel soon enough. He would have Beatrix and Lanthimos to deal with at the very least. Cassius, he hoped, was still safely sealed away.

But Shane was not about to trust fate when it came to Beatrix any longer. He had to be ready for everything.

The dark roads gave way to the headlights as Shane got closer to his target. He traveled side roads when he could, staying away from anyone who might see him or remember the car.

He didn't plan to cause a scene when he got where he was going, but he had every reason to believe things were about to get ugly.

CHAPTER 24

RISE AND DIE

The Motor Court Inn was an ugly little horseshoe-shaped motel about five miles from the nearest town border. The ancient sign up front advertised that it had air conditioning and HBO, something that might have been worthy of attention in the nineties. The place looked like it had been built in the sixties and was about as ugly as any motel Shane had seen.

There was a strange castle motif to everything, and the roof had crenellations for some reason. A big, neon vacancy sign blazed under the name of the motel, and Shane drove past without pulling into the lot, scanning the vehicles instead.

Beatrix's SUV was parked toward the rear of the lot, to the right edge of the horseshoe shape. There were three other cars, but none were close to the SUV.

Shane pulled off to the side of the road so his car couldn't be seen from any of the motel windows. He walked back in the dark with August and checked out the area from behind the pole that held up the motel sign.

Lights were on in the main office, but the windows were covered by blinds. Shane could see no shadows moving inside, but the light flickered rapidly, which gave the impression someone was inside watching television.

None of the rooms had lights on, so Shane assumed all the temporary residents were sleeping. Beatrix and her partner had been there for a couple of hours at most. He wasn't convinced that they were asleep; it seemed more Beatrix's style that one of them would be awake. Hell, based on his experience, one of them was probably watching him already.

They waited for several minutes until Shane was confident that no one was likely to be up and moving about. He circled to the far side of the horseshoe, staying in the dark between the road and the motel, and then headed toward the SUV.

"I need you to go ahead and see what room they're in," Shane said. Beatrix could have parked the SUV in the wrong place as a precaution.

August did as he was told without complaint. He drifted into the walls of the nearest room and was gone for several minutes. When he returned, he was two doors down from the SUV. Room fourteen was the one he flagged, and he gestured to the next one as well. Fourteen and fifteen. Beatrix wanted her privacy.

Shane approached, sticking to the shadows as much as he could. August met him at the bend in the horseshoe.

"She's in fourteen and Lanthimos is in fifteen," he explained. "Looks like they're both asleep."

"Looks like?" Shane asked.

"Covers are pulled up, no noise, no movement."

"Cassius?"

August gestured to room fourteen.

"There's a box on the nightstand next to the bed. Different from the one Mr. Winston had, but close enough. It's still sealed, so he must be inside. I didn't see any ghosts."

Shane nodded and August moved as if he was ready to go, stopping when he saw that Shane wasn't going anywhere.

"What's wrong?" the ghost asked.

"Smells wrong," he replied. "This is all coming together very easily."

"Easy? They buried you alive," the ghost said.

"Yeah, they did. They could have killed me outright, but they didn't."

"Yes, because she's horrible. She wanted you to suffer. If Phelps hadn't been there to rescue you, you would have suffocated in that box."

"If Phelps hadn't been there, I would have. But she left Phelps there, too."

"To die," August added.

"Did she check his pulse?" Shane asked.

"What?"

"Before they left. Did Beatrix or her partner check to see if Phelps was alive?"

"No," August said.

"Right. They didn't care. This seems very much like a game. Maybe we live, maybe we die, no difference. She's just having fun."

"You think she's in there waiting for us?" August asked.

"I do," Shane answered.

It was hard to get into Beatrix's mind. Shane realized that was because she thought about things in a counterintuitive way. She wasn't planning specific outcomes; she was open to whatever happened. She dug a grave just in case Shane showed up. If he hadn't, she probably wouldn't have given him another thought. She would fight Cassius, take Phelps' money, and be done with it.

Shane got a feeling that she hadn't expected him to show up at the motel, but she wouldn't be surprised if he did. Maybe it would happen; maybe it wouldn't. The play was what thrilled her, not the outcome.

The way Beatrix behaved didn't jibe with how she conducted business. Knowing who Shane was, knowing about Cassius. There was a disconnect between her flagrant attitude and her wealth of knowledge. Someone else had to be feeding her information, Shane couldn't reconcile the way she worked otherwise. She was the brawn and someone else was the brains. That or she had drastic personality shifts.

If she expected him or had at least prepared for him, then he had to realize things would not be as easy as walking in and stealing the lead-lined box with Cassius inside. On the other hand, what if that was what she *wasn't* expecting?

Shane's instinct was to find another way into the room. To go through maybe the bathroom window, do something that would surprise Beatrix and get the drop on her. But if she expected all of that, none of it would work. She would be prepared for Shane to spring something like that on her.

"So, what do we do?" August asked.

"We take what we came for," Shane said.

He wouldn't use any gimmicks or any tricks on Beatrix. Instead, he would just steal the box. If it worked, he'd have what he needed. If it didn't, he would have to beat Beatrix, and he expected that, anyway. At least this way was up front and on his terms.

"Unlock the door."

August opened the door from inside and Shane went in. The room was as small and ugly as he'd expected. The light from the parking lot filtered into the room and illuminated the bed enough to show the covers on top of Beatrix as she slept with her back to the door.

Shane's eyes went to the nightstand and the lead-lined box. He crept toward it, careful to make no sound on the floor, and picked it up quickly and quietly. He held it close like he was carrying a football and turned to leave.

But something nagged at the back of Shane's mind. Even if Beatrix had planned for him to come through the bathroom window or some other stealthy route, she would not have been sleeping when he got there.

He looked at the bed and the form under the covers, and felt his stomach drop. August had not looked closely at the bed.

Shane pulled back the covers. Pillows and a bag of clothes along with a blonde wig were lumped up under the blanket. There was no one there. There had never been anyone there.

He turned and made his way to the door. Two whole steps and Beatrix was there, leaning against the front end of the SUV with a big smile.

"You're alive!" she said in mock surprise. "Great!"

"And so are you. Damn," he replied.

"Oh, I'm going to live forever, Solo. Barely broke a sweat out there. But you damn near broke your skull. Are you sure you're cut out for this? Maybe you oughtta start feeding ghost pigeons in the park."

She pushed off the SUV and walked toward him until they were face to face, so close that he could smell her sweat.

"You want to give me that box now?" she asked.

"Not really," he began. Beatrix's knee came up into his groin, and Shane stumbled back a step and collapsed, dropping the box. He landed on his knees, and she punched down hard, hitting the wound on his head and causing his vision to blank for a moment as he fell flat at her feet.

"Most of my questions are rhetorical, Solo," she told him, kicking him in the gut.

Shane grunted and waited for her to strike again. He caught her foot and rolled with her, causing her to go off-balance and fall next to him.

She landed on her back in the parking lot and kicked out immediately, taking Shane in the ribs with enough force to make him grunt. He caught her ankle as she pulled it back, punching her twice in the thigh and the side of her knee.

Beatrix laughed through the groans of pain. Shane was back on his knees as she got up. He was faster this time, knocking her arms out and forcing her to her stomach as he planted an elbow in her kidneys and then punched her in the face.

She laughed again and managed to clip Shane with another kick to the gut. They traded blows, each one landing strong hits that bruised or cut flesh. No matter how much she bled, Beatrix continued to laugh.

Shane took another kick to the face and caught her leg again. He held it and struck her knee, aiming to break it to prevent any further attacks and ensure she couldn't escape. Something flew past his face and hit the SUV behind him before he followed through. Beatrix had thrown the box.

The box splintered, and the latch broke as it fell to the ground. The old straight razor tumbled out and Cassius was there, balanced on one broken leg above them.

Shane was closer to the ghost. There was no pause again, and no need to orient himself. Cassius plucked Shane from the ground by his collar and swung, slamming him face-first into the SUV.

Shane felt his nose crunch and a spray of blood burst out. The ghost repeated the maneuver and was winding back for a third when Shane hooked an arm around Cassius' broken leg and pulled as hard as he could.

Cassius crumpled, losing his grip on Shane. Shane reached out, grabbing the first thing he could get his hands on, and found himself grasping a handful of limp, greasy hair that felt like cold, wet thread. He twisted his fingers into it and pulled back sharply, tearing a chunk of the ghost's scalp from his head.

The ghost howled and Shane scrambled on top of him, slamming his fists into the spirit's mouth, loosening teeth with each blow until they began to crack and collapse down his throat.

Cassius growled and sputtered but was not forming words. He grabbed at Shane when and where he could but gave up each time Shane landed another blow.

Shane's fists were like pistons. There was no style in his attack, and it was not as forceful or planned as it could have been. He sacrificed accuracy and strategy for speed, wanting to keep the ghost busy and on the defense.

Or that's what he told himself. In truth, he just wanted to beat Cassius. Shane would punch him until his head collapsed if he had to.

He held Cassius' head down with one hand, gripping the limp, greasy hair, and used the other to pound his fists into the dead man's face. Over and over and over, he slammed his knuckles into dead flesh and phantom bone. Cassius could only endure so much.

"Save some of that energy for me, Solo," Beatrix chirped. The toe of her boot clipped Shane in the chin, and his head snapped back. She stood over him and laughed.

"You didn't think you were going to live through this, did you?"

CHAPTER 25

FINAL HARVEST

The laughter angered Shane more than the beating. He was growing a hatred for Beatrix's voice. Just the sound of it grated on his nerves.

Her foot connected with his stomach and pain flared to his back. The beating was painful as well, but the fact she wouldn't shut up while she was doing it was more than he could bear.

He felt Cassius' hands grabbing him from the other side. His vision was blurring, and every time he got up, Beatrix knocked him down again. He spat blood on her leg as he deflected a kick and tried to counter.

"You're still trying. You need to learn to accept your fate, Solo. Just let me kill you. Let me watch that little spark in your eyes fizzle out. Stop being so goddamn stubborn."

She kicked him in the chest, and he thought he felt a rib snap. The blow created a new tightness in his chest and made it hard to breathe. Shane wheezed and rolled away. She laughed at him again and stepped on his arm, holding him in place.

"Look at you," she said, leaning down so they were eye to eye. "So sad. I'm going to kill you now, okay?"

She righted herself and raised her foot. Shane stared up at the heel of her boot and lifted his other arm to catch it before it made contact.

Beatrix produced one final laugh but before she brought her foot down, August was at her side. Shane watched the ghost grab her head and scream in her face. She screamed back, and for a moment, Shane didn't understand what was happening until blood spattered on the ground next to him. He watched as August pulled off her right ear and threw it behind him.

Beatrix doubled over, holding her hands to the side of her head. August took her by the hair, smashing her face into the side of the SUV the same way Cassius had done to Shane moments earlier.

Shane couldn't help but laugh. Beatrix and August moved out of his range of vision, and he lay there on the ground for a moment, catching his breath. Cassius' hand clumsily grabbed at him again, and he pulled away, rolling over to face the big ghost.

He had not destroyed Cassius, but he had destroyed his face worse than what had happened to Phelps. Most of his skull had collapsed inward, and few recognizable human features remained. His nose and his mouth were destroyed, replaced by pulpy, bone sludge, and Shane could only make out one eye.

Shane awkwardly got to his feet, using the precious few moments he had to steady himself and catch his breath. Cassius was doing the same, wobbling on his broken leg and undeterred by his ruined face. His one eye fixed on Shane, and the broken cavern of his mouth produced a wet growl.

"You're not getting away from me this time," Shane said.

The ghost spoke, or at least Shane thought he did. None of the sounds were discernible as words. Whatever happened, Shane had ended the ghost's talking days. Realizing he couldn't say anything, Cassius gave up and lurched toward Shane. He didn't need a voice to make his intentions known. He wanted Shane dead as much as Beatrix did.

Shane slipped his hand into his pocket as he waited on the ghost. No need to waste energy walking to meet him. He felt the cold iron of the rings against his fingers and slipped one on, pushing it down the length of his index finger within the pocket.

He heard Beatrix scream behind him. August was still fighting her and still holding his own. He had finally been pushed far enough. Or maybe he just realized the alternative. Better late than never, Shane figured.

Cassius lumbered forward on his ruined leg. His one eye was

bloodshot and grim. It didn't look like he could blink anymore, but the eye was fixed on Shane, and the hatred was plain.

"You look like ground beef," Shane said, taunting the ghost. "Remember all that tough guy talk before? Eating people, whatever that crap was about? Now here you are looking like an overpriced appetizer at a French restaurant. Cassius tartare."

He laughed as obnoxiously as he could. The ghost came at him faster, ignoring his injury and lunging. The sound Cassius produced was bestial, and he reached for Shane with his arms extended.

Shane punched him square in his broken mess of a face. The iron ring on his finger collided with the pulpy mass, and Cassius was gone in a blink, thrust back to his haunted item.

The transfer took no time. It was an instantaneous change of position, but Shane was ready. He turned sharply to face the box where it had fallen after Beatrix threw it. Cassius appeared, his back to Shane, standing over the straight razor in the parking lot.

Shane took the ghost to the ground from behind with a kick to the back of his broken leg. Cassius collapsed and Shane followed him down. He plunged a fist into the broken face while steadying the ghost's head with his other hand. His hands came together swiftly and forcefully, crushing Cassius' head between them.

The explosion was one of the most powerful Shane had endured. His body shot backward like he had been hit by a car. He landed hard in the paved lot and grunted as his head smacked the flat surface, sending a new wave of debilitating pain through his body.

"Shane!"

He groaned. August was desperately calling for him. Shane felt like he could sleep for a week, but the job was not done. He needed to finish off Beatrix.

Shane sat up and saw her then, in front of the motel room, with August in front of her. The ghost was missing his left hand, and she had returned the favor of losing her ear by taking his.

She waited until she knew that Shane could see her. The ghost said nothing more. Her hands twisted and pulled, wrenching August's head from his shoulders and crushing it.

His body burst and vanished in the expulsion of energy. It caused Beatrix to stumble, but she retained her footing. The barest trace of the explosion reached Shane, and further away, by where he had parked Phelps' car, a twin explosion followed. Then it was gone. Only he and Beatrix remained.

"You have no idea how much you just pissed me off, Solo," she shouted. "Cassius was mine. That was my hunt!"

"Sue me," he said. He got to his feet, keeping his eyes on her. The side of her face was awash in blood from her missing ear. August must have gotten some other good hits in as well. Her left eye was swollen, and her nose bled freely. At least August went out fighting.

They stared at each other. Blood was splattered across the parking lot and the SUV. The lead-lined box was shattered, the result of the straight razor's destruction.

"I'm going to get my money's worth," she told him. He shrugged.

"You talk too much."

"You breathe too much," she countered.

He approached her then, and she waited for him, standing in the doorway to the motel room. Her eyes were fixed on Shane as he closed the gap between them, but he saw her look to his right at the last minute.

Shane turned, too slow to react as Lanthimos emerged from the far side of the SUV. He cracked Shane in the side of the head with the butt of his gun, knocking him to the ground.

Shane cursed in his head and then out loud as the man began kicking him. He pummeled Shane, hitting him in the gut, ribs, and face. His vision swam, and he blacked out, only to wake up to still being kicked.

He got to his feet, but the other man was uninjured and not close to being tired. He slammed Shane in the back of the head where he'd already been struck countless times. The world went black.

Shane woke with the taste of blood and dirt in his mouth. A distant siren screeched wildly, the sound merging with the drumming in Shane's skull.

A hand grabbed his face and lifted it from the ground. Shane looked up at Beatrix crouching in front of him. She held his chin firmly and stared into his eyes.

"You have no idea what you cost me," she said. "Cassius was mine. Even your little friend was meant to be mine, but not like this. Not in some goddamn parking lot. This wasn't a hunt. There was no challenge. You cost me two. Two!"

"Good," Shane groaned, smiling as best as he could. Beatrix smiled back.

"It won't be good. Not for you. I'm not going to kill you. Not here, anyway. Not now. You're going to heal. You're going to get better because I want you strong, Solo. I want you ready and confident and cocky, just like you were when we met. Just like when you thought you'd never end up here with your head busted open like an egg, only alive because I let you live. You owe every second of your life to me from now on, until I snatch it from you. I own you. I am your god now; do you understand? You live because I let you."

She dropped his face into the dirt, and he stayed there, breathing heavily. He was too sore to get up.

"I will come to collect, Solo. Don't think for a second this is done."

He heard her footsteps crunching across the gravel on the pavement as she walked away. He heard a car door close a moment later, and then the engine started. He didn't look where she was going. It didn't matter. This time, she'd be gone until she wanted to be found again. No doubt, she'd already removed the tracker from the vehicle.

The sirens drew closer. Shane took long, awkward breaths that hurt his chest. His mouth was full of dirt and blood, and he pushed it out with his tongue but couldn't roll over. His head throbbed, the pain close to unbearable. He heard footsteps coming toward him.

"Oh my God, can you hear me?" a voice asked. It sounded like an older man, no one Shane recognized. Maybe another ghost, or the desk clerk. It didn't matter.

He grunted. It was the best he could do to prove he was alive. The stranger told him that help was on the way. He told him that they had called the police and an ambulance.

Flashing lights on the paved driveway indicated that someone had arrived.

"Here! This guy needs a doctor quickly!" the stranger shouted.

There were more voices, but Shane couldn't pay attention to what everyone was saying. He felt hands touching, and then he blacked out again. When he opened his eyes again, he was on his back and looking up at the ceiling of an ambulance. A paramedic checked him over and asked him questions. Shane couldn't understand the words and closed his eyes.

He was in a hospital the next time he opened his eyes. A doctor and several nurses were around him. He could hear monitors beeping, and he had a tube in his nose. Every inch of his body felt bruised. Breathing was difficult, even with the tube in his nose. He tried to focus on what people said but gave up. He didn't care. They knew what they were doing. They'd take care of it, or they wouldn't. Nothing he could say would help.

Shane wasn't sure how much time passed before he was aware of his surroundings again. He was in a room this time, and the doctors were gone. There was still a beeping machine, but things seemed less hurried and less intense. He sat up and groaned.

"Relax, Ryan," a familiar voice said. Someone approached his bedside, and Shane focused his eyes.

"Ventura?" he said, his throat feeling dry, and his voice strained.

"Yeah," the FBI agent said. "What the hell were you doing?"

"Getting beaten to death in a parking lot," he answered. "You?"

"Waiting for an email alert about friends getting beaten to death. What the hell happened?"

"Did you not hear the beaten-to-death part?"

Ventura scoffed.

"Is this what you had me looking into? The Harvesters?"

"Yeah," Shane said. "I caught up with them."

"You need to tell me what you know. I can track these people down, and we can end these hunts. At the very least, we have them on theft, assault, attempted murder, and murder. Doesn't matter if ghosts are involved; they'll go down for this."

"No thanks," Shane said, closing his eyes again.

"No thanks?" Ventura said incredulously. "What the hell does that mean?"

"I've got this one. I'll find them," he answered.

"You almost died," Ventura said.

Shane grunted.

"Yeah. She made the mistake of not finishing what she started. I won't."

EPILOGUE

Mill River High School had been abandoned for close to ten years. The school district had been rezoned, and three other districts had merged. The student population was shuffled off to other schools with lower densities than the state mandated.

Three schools closed, one new school was built, and everyone was operating at capacity in the end. Mill River was the first to close and the largest of the three. Nothing had been done with the land since it had shut down because the state couldn't decide what it wanted to do with the property.

Everyone knew the school would be torn down because there was little anyone could do with an old school. That meant rezoning and more money to pay for it, and then deciding what to do with the land afterward. That and a dozen other problems that most people in the area had long since stopped caring about.

In the meantime, the school had become a favorite spot for former students. The exterior had endured its fair share of vandalism, but the inside had been almost completely repainted with graffiti and various other tags. Most of the windows had been broken, the lights had been destroyed, and someone had even taken most of the toilets. A few were still in the yard by the basketball nets, having been thrown off the roof.

Much of the damage was done in the first year after the school closed. After that, people slowly stopped going there. Rumors about a ghost in the building soon followed and, while no one believed them, no one challenged them, either. Everyone knew someone who swore they saw or heard something in the school that couldn't be explained.

Caleb's older brother, Jason, had been a student at Mill River and had also partied there after the school closed. Caleb had gone to Bowden starting with his freshman year and had never experienced Mill River. He just saw it every day when he passed it on the way home.

Jason was one of the people who insisted there was a ghost at Mill River. More than once, he told the story of breaking in after prom—which took place at Bowden—and having a party with his friends. There was beer and music, and then, just after midnight, something shut off the power. Jason said all he saw was a shadow, but it passed through doors and pushed someone out of a window. He swore it was real.

Caleb didn't believe a word of his brother's story. Jason had told him so many lies growing up that it was hard to recall a thing his brother had ever said that was verifiably true. Caleb did believe they'd had a party at the school, and he also believed, as his own graduation loomed, that it would be a good place to gather a lot of people without local parents or cops getting in the way and being a pain.

The only way to know for sure if it was a suitable place to party was to break in and party there. He got four friends to agree to try it out and, just after eleven on a Saturday night, he cut the lock off a rear door, and broke in.

The rear of Mill River faced the woods, so there was no way for nosy neighbors to ruin the fun. Once the lock was cut, the group filtered into the school, which was in much better condition than Caleb had expected.

He had heard it was trashed. There was a lot of graffiti, but the hallways were clean. There was no junk or broken glass as he'd been led to believe. Another lie from his brother.

"This place smells weird," his friend Alicia said.

"Just dampness," Mark replied. "Mildew, I guess."

"Yeah, and it stinks," Alicia said.

"Whatever. We can find a room with open windows or something," Bekka said.

She tried the first door on their left and popped into what had been a classroom. Now, it was empty except for a pair of broken desks. The windows were broken but boarded up, ending the hopes of airflow to cut through the smell.

"There's nowhere to sit," Derek said. "Let's find the cafeteria or something."

The group ventured deeper into the old high school, opening doors and looking across empty rooms covered in spray paint.

The place grew repetitive and uninteresting. No one wanted to stand around and drink beer in a place that smelled like an unclean locker room. The floor was an option, but no one wanted to try that, either. They could just as easily have had a party in the woods and sat on old logs or lawn chairs.

"This place kind of sucks, Caleb," Alicia said.

"Yeah," he agreed.

While he never believed the ghost story, he thought at least the part about the party must have been true. It sounded like a lot of fun, but he couldn't imagine anyone having a good time in an empty classroom. It was boring, and there was nothing to do. Maybe his brother's idea of a fun party was a lot different from his.

Just when it seemed like there were no redeeming features at Mill River, Mark opened the door to the second-floor teacher's lounge and laughed from the hallway.

"Now, this looks like it might work," he said.

The others crowded around to see. The room was not as large as a classroom, but it was carpeted and still fully furnished, with two sofas and a dozen chairs around round tables. The room was still clean, and the previous vandals had left it inexplicably untouched.

The group settled in quickly. Bekka opened a window that looked out over the old parking lot, and Alicia poured a drink before taking a seat on the nearest sofa. Caleb took a beer from the small cooler they had brought, and the five settled into talking and laughing, lounging on the surprisingly comfortable couches that had been left behind.

No more than five minutes had passed, and Derek was setting up shots of Fireball, when the sound of a door closing loudly elsewhere in the school echoed through the hallways.

Caleb froze and turned toward the teacher's lounge door. The others shut up immediately and waited in anticipation.

"What was that?" Bekka whispered.

Alicia shushed her. Hinges creaked somewhere as another door opened and then immediately slammed shut.

Alicia covered her mouth, muffling a surprised scream. Caleb looked at Derek and then Mark. More hinges wailed, followed by another slamming door.

"We have to get out of here," Mark whispered.

Caleb shook his head. They needed to be quiet.

Another door slammed. Someone was checking every door, making their way down a hallway.

"They're getting closer," Bekka whispered, her voice shaky.

She wasn't wrong. Each slammed door sounded a little louder and closer than the last. Caleb still couldn't tell which direction it came from. The lounge was closer to one end of the hall than the other, but if someone was out there, they'd be seen if they ran off. Only one exterior door was unlocked, and it was on the far side of the building.

"You think it's a security guard or something?" Derek asked.

"Does this place look like it has a security guard?" Alicia shot back.

"Then what? Cops?"

No one had an answer. It could have been the police. If someone had watched them wander onto the property and not come back out, they could have easily deduced that the group had broken in. But if it was the police, why weren't they saying anything? Why weren't they calling for them to come out and show themselves?

"It's probably some other idiots," Caleb suggested. "Someone saw the broken lock and is just messing around."

"Or it's a ghost," Derek suggested.

"Slamming doors?" Alicia countered.

"Hell yes, slamming doors. That's what ghosts do."

"Ghosts aren't real," Caleb said.

It had to be some other teenagers. They had told others at school they were going there; it wasn't a secret mission or anything. People knew they'd be at Mill River. It was probably Davis or Carter or some of the guys from the football team.

"It's gotta be someone from school," Caleb added. "Someone is messing with us."

The next slam was louder than it should have been. Whoever it was had skipped some doors and gotten much closer. Caleb couldn't stop himself from jumping, surprised by the volume and closeness.

"Screw this," he said, heading for the door.

"Caleb, what the hell?" Bekka said, her voice almost a hiss.

"I'm going to see who it is," he told her.

He approached the door and then stopped as, slowly, the door opened on its own. When they had entered the room, the door had been quiet, but now, the hinges produced a drawn-out, high-pitched squeal as the door moved with an almost impossible slowness.

Caleb froze just a few paces away with his friends behind him. The hallway beyond the door was too dark to see anything. It opened into blackness and, as Caleb watched, the shadows seemed to ooze into the room.

Darkness flowed like water across the carpet and began to creep up the walls. It was like watching a stop motion of someone painting. It crept up and out, the blackness enveloping the walls and the carpet, and concealing everything behind it.

Caleb retreated to the far corner of the room, and the others moved with him. As they moved back, a figure emerged from the center of the darkness. It was shaped like a man, but it walked with an awkward, pronounced limp.

As the form came into the light that the teens had brought with them, Caleb heard some of the others gasp. Bekka let out a quiet scream, and either Derek or Mark simply said the word, "No."

The thing that Caleb was looking at could not have been alive. It was rotten, with bone and slimy green-and-black muscle visible through putrid flesh. It was a walking corpse, as impossible a thing as that was.

Even though his friends had backed into the corner, Caleb couldn't make his legs work. Seeing the thing had caused his brain to stop functioning for a minute as he tried to understand how he could be watching the dead walk.

The school's old, rancid smell was not mildew; it was the dead thing shambling toward them. It smelled stagnant and earthy and foul. It was the smell of things that had died on top of other things.

"Jesus…" The word was a whisper, and it was all he could manage as terror turned his muscles to mush.

The rotten creature's green, goopy flesh glistened and hung from the bones and skull like it might fall off at any moment. It had no eyes, but Caleb could feel its gaze on him. It saw him, as sure as he saw it.

He didn't realize that Bekka was screaming at first. He was still having a hard time comprehending what he saw.

The creature took another step. It was within arm's reach of Caleb, and it lifted its arm. Caleb wanted to back away, but he couldn't make his body listen to his thoughts. He was going to die.

The shadows in the doorway behind the creature wavered as a single flame sprang to life. Caleb watched in confusion as a bald man lit a cigarette and tucked an old Zippo lighter into his pocket. The man grabbed the rotten monster by the shoulder and yanked it backward, pulling it away from Caleb and back into the hallway.

Bekka's screams subsided, and Derek grabbed Caleb, pulling him back.

"Are you okay?" he said, his voice panicked and rushed.

"What the hell just happened?" he replied.

"Who cares? Let's just go," Alicia demanded. She pushed past him toward the door.

Caleb could move again. He felt the fear replaced with adrenaline and a strong need to run far and fast. He followed Alicia to the door.

The bald man was on top of the monster in the hall. He ripped off one of its arms and threw it away. It hit the ground and clattered for a moment before vanishing.

"What the hell is going on?" Caleb muttered.

Alicia was already gone, and Bekka was following with Derek. Only Mark remained, encouraging Caleb to come with him.

"Who the hell cares, Caleb? Come on!"

The bald man turned his head and looked Caleb dead in the eye. He was badly bruised like he'd been in a serious fight recently. He pulled the cigarette from his mouth and pointed at Caleb.

"Listen to your friend, kid. You should go," he advised.

Caleb nodded dumbly and began to stumble away. The bald man returned his attention to the monster beneath him.

"I know Beatrix released you. Tell me about the Harvesters," the man said, breaking the fingers off the monster's hand.

The creature began to speak, its voice a wet, low growl. Caleb turned and ran, not wanting to see or hear what came next.

Check out these best-selling series from our talented authors:

GHOST STORIES

RON RIPLEY
BERKLEY STREET SERIES
MOVING IN SERIES
HAUNTED COLLECTION SERIES
DEATH HUNTER SERIES

IAN FORTEY
JIGSAW OF SOULS SERIES
CULT OF THE ENDLESS NIGHT SERIES

SUPERNATURAL SUSPENSE

A. I. NASSER
SLAUGHTER SERIES
SIN SERIES

DAVID LONGHORN
NIGHTMARE SERIES
ASYLUM SERIES

SARA CLANCY
THE BELL WITCH SERIES
BANSHEE SERIES

For a complete list of our new releases and best-selling horror books, visit
ScareStreet.com or scan the QR code below!

www.ingramcontent.com/pod-product-compliance
Lightning Source LLC
Chambersburg PA
CBHW050345030726
47503CB00008B/2628